CW01629175

His Ample Desire

Terri Mackenzie

Copyright © 2024 by Terri Mackenzie

All rights reserved.

No part of this publication may be reproduced, distributed, or transmitted in any form or by any means, including photocopying, recording, or other electronic or mechanical methods, without the prior written permission of the publisher, except as permitted by U.S. copyright law.

The story, all names, characters, and incidents portrayed in this production are fictitious. No identification with actual persons (living or deceased), places, buildings, and products is intended or should be inferred.

Book Cover by GetCovers.

Also by Terri Mackenzie

Finders Keepers

In Search of a Hero

To Marry the Devil

The Picture of Desire

His Ample Desire

To Have and to Hold

To Steal a Bride

Later in Life

The Spinster's Seduction

Contents

Prologue

April 1815

George Comerford wrapped his hand around the front of Caroline Spenser's throat, the possessiveness of the gesture sending delicious heat through her body as he pushed her front against the library wall. "Now," he murmured in her ear, one hand at the fall of his breeches. He fumbled a little as he freed himself, and Caroline hoisted her dress further out of the way. They had perhaps ten minutes before they risked being discovered, and, as always, that risk of discovery added an edge to her pleasure. Frantic, hot, beyond the point of no return.

This was how she preferred to conduct her liaisons: with breathless urgency. She had never been one to submit to a man making love to her—there was nothing of love in what she did.

Gentleman had one thing and one thing alone to offer, and it was entirely unconnected to the heart.

The thing George Comerford had to offer pressed against the flesh of her buttocks, parting her cheeks and sliding between and through to enter her from behind. Already slick, she groaned as he pushed, and he cursed. The hand that wasn't on her throat came to splay on her stomach, holding her in place against him, and she found she liked the possessiveness. This was the first time he had asserted his dominance in quite that way, and she was more than happy to yield to the commands of his body.

Two days ago, she had not so much as met George Comerford; when they left for London once more in twelve days, there was an unspoken agreement that whatever this was would come to an end. While she was there at Worthington Hall, however, she hoped they would continue to do *this* as frequently as possible.

He hissed another curse in her ear and tightened his hold on her throat. She arched her back, tipping her head back until it rested on his shoulder, and gave herself over to him.

Chapter One

May 1815

"How is he?" George asked as he divested himself of his hat and gloves in the front hall. Forbes, the elderly butler his father had insisted on transplanting to Bath, inclined his head.

"The waters have been helping, sir."

George bit back his grimace with difficulty. He had only tasted Bath's famous waters once, and it had been enough to convince him that they could not be of any help. But if his father believed in them, then by all means he would let it continue. "Is he well enough to see me?" he asked.

"I shall inform him of your arrival, sir."

"I'll wait in the library." Steps idle, he strolled into the house's mediocre library. When he had been at Cambridge, he had thrown himself into his studies with unbecoming enthusiasm, and it had taken years for him to improve his reputation.

When no one else was around, however, he allowed himself a moment to appreciate the grandeur that was literature. Not merely the fashionable quotes to produce to his fellows, but the sheer wonder that accompanied the collection of ideas. At thirteen, he had used to lie on the floor of his father's study and read Shakespeare, marvelling at the use of language.

Now, however, as he dragged his fingers along the leather spines, his reflection on the noble art was interrupted by far less noble thoughts. In essence, ones of a certain lady whom he had pushed up against shelves similar to this. Her breasts against the books, her head half turned so he could see the hectic flush on her pretty cheeks, her skirts around her wide hips.

Forbes entered the room with a slight bow. "Your father is ready to see you, sir."

Clearing his throat, George nodded and waved for the butler to lead the way. The townhouse was narrow and tall, and they climbed two sets of stairs before finally coming to his father's room. It was by far the nicest in the house, but it was a fool's choice to situate himself upstairs when his health had declined.

Forbes opened the door with a murmured "Mr Comerford here to see you, my lord", and closed it behind George the moment he stepped in.

The room was darkened, burnt sage hanging in the air, and the curtains pulled close. In the armchair by the fire, sitting bolt upright despite his shaking hands, was his father.

George's first instinct was to pity the man. Benjamin Comerford, Viscount Worthington, was a proud man, and had in his prime been known as an excellent hunter and bruising rider. Now he was a gaunt shadow of his former self, burning sage to keep the spirits away, though when healthy he would have derided the existence of such things.

Then his father fastened him with an icy glare that time had not diluted, and his pity melted into something hotter like anger. Resentment.

Hardly surprising: their relationship over the years had been strained at best.

"You should try opening a window," he remarked as he strolled forwards, taking the seat opposite his father. "I find fresh air does wonders when one is feeling under the weather."

His father's bony hands tightened around his handkerchief, and George noticed that the white material was stained red.

"How goes your search?" the Viscount asked, voice scratchy and weak. "Have you found a suitable wife yet?"

"How delightful that we are not even to exchange pleasantries before getting into it."

"I do not have time for pleasantries," his father said. Once, when he was a boy, George recalled his father being almost good-tempered.

Ah, heady days. Long in the past now.

"I have not yet made my choice," George said, crossing his legs. "Be assured when I do, I will let you know."

"You're confident of being received well?"

"I expect so. Unless she's in love with another."

"Bah," his father said. "Love."

"Quite," George drawled. If he could have contrived to marry for love, he would have done, but he thought it was unlikely he would be so lucky. In recent years, the only lady to have captured his attention for more than a few weeks had made it plain she had no interest in marriage.

"You've been dragging your feet too long. Pick a girl and have done with it." His father hacked and coughed. "I don't have time for your dilly-dallying."

Keeping his irritation from his face, George removed his snuffbox from his coat pocket and inhaled a pinch. It had the rather pleasing consequence of inducing his father to scowl, so he did so again. "You know I owe it to the family name to choose the right lady," he said lazily.

His father's eyes narrowed, but as this was a sentiment he had himself said several months ago, he could find nothing to object to.

"But I hardly see the rush," he continued. "I'm thirty, hardly an old man yet. Give me time, Father."

"Time for what? Am I to pass from this world having not seen my son married?" He tapped his stick impatiently against the carpet. "I think not. I will have Forbes write you a list of families I consider eligible. Pick one. And soon."

"I take it you have nothing else to say to me?"

"Not until you find a wife."

"Charmed." He gave a mocking bow. "I shall see myself out."

"I mean it, George. My patience is running thin."

"This was, as always, a productive meeting, Father." George reached the door and had almost escaped before his father sighed.

"If you would not do it to oblige me, do it in memory of your mother. She would have wanted this."

What a vilely low blow. George shut the door with a slam and leaned against it, dragging a hand down his face. While his relationship with his father was strained, he had adored his mother until the day she died, several years ago.

Well, he'd known this day was coming, whether he liked it or not.

"Good day, Forbes," he said as he descended the stairs again. "I'll see myself out. I believe you shall be instructed to shortly send me a list of eligible brides."

The butler inclined his head regally. "Very good, sir."

If only, George thought wryly, it was.

Caroline read the letter in her hand, a crease forming between her brows. After a few moments, she reached up and pressed her fingers against the groove, smoothing it out again. Her looks were her primary currency, and she couldn't afford for something as trifling as a little destitution to hurry time along. This was, after all, nothing particularly new. Ever since her husband's untimely death, she had been accustomed to living life somewhat . . . precariously.

And now this additional call on her purse.

We received no answer to our last missive, so forgive my impertinence in writing again. You are behind on your payments for Jacqueline, and there is the matter of her dowry. You understand that we will be presenting her next year, and if she is to take, she must have a sizeable dowry.

We await your response.

There was no signature. Mrs Smith rarely left her name at the bottom of her letters; she had consented to accept Jacqueline as her own, to give her a home and a roof over her head and clothes on her back—for a price, always for a price—but she did not approve of Caroline.

Then again, few did approve of a girl who had lain with a man outside of marriage, conceived his bastard, and given the child away.

Her father had been the one to negotiate the arrangement, and when he had died almost ten years ago now, Caroline had taken over the monthly payments. After her husband's death—he had left his fortune elsewhere—it had been a struggle, but she had contrived it.

The matter of the dowry, however.

Caroline sucked at her teeth.

Usually, when she worried about going short, she would dip her pen into ink and write a cajoling letter to the man—or men—paying for the delights of her company, requesting a gift.

Usually, these gentlemen obliged and after an appropriate amount of time, she could sell his gift and send the money into the country.

Usually, she had a gentleman on which to call.

That made today's letter particularly inconvenient.

"My lady," her butler said. "The carriage has arrived."

She stuffed the letter back in her reticule and forced a smile. Despite her somewhat dubious reputation, her birth and marriage were good enough that most hosts still invited her. Of course, Lady Jersey was never going to permit her an Almack's voucher, but there were worse things: she was not a mere girl in her first Season, after all. And Almack's had always struck her as singularly *dull.* One could not so much as sneak a kiss.

She might use her lovers to fund her obligations, but she did enjoy her escapades, for the most part. The dowagers lining the walls tonight would be shocked at the idea that Caroline, for all her veneer of respectability, *enjoyed* being a man's mistress.

Ah well, if she was selling her soul, she had best make the most of it.

The carriage was dark, but the journey was short, and when she finally pulled up outside Lady Peterborough's grand townhouse, her curls were fluffed, her bosom was plumped and she was at full advantage in a daring red gown and white gloves.

A small, infinitely girlish part of her marvelled at the lights and beauty, and the simple gallantry of the footmen as they took her coat. Despite knowing better, that part of her hadn't died when she moved to the metropolis. There was something delightful about beauty; she should know, as a connoisseur.

Lady Peterborough, smiling and vaguely polite, greeted her with a press of her hands before turning her attention to the next guests. Caroline moved into the ballroom, the heat stifling and a buzz of expectation in the air. So long as she did not lose her nerve, as she had done every time she'd attended a ball these past five weeks, she would secure her future.

"Caroline," Mr Isaac Barnaby called out to her, attracting her attention with a flick of his fingers. "Come, have some wine." He smiled as he handed her the glass, his fingers brushing hers. "I haven't seen you in a while, my dear. I've missed you."

Ordinarily, she would say she missed him too—and perhaps she would have meant it—if she had not been distracted by the recollection of a certain gentleman. One with the mouth of a poet and the hands of a sinner.

Annoyed with herself, she sighed inwardly. Anyone would think she was a naive girl in the first flush of youth enjoying her first seduction—and inevitable heartbreak. She would not let that happen again.

"Darling," she said, accepting the wine. "You can hardly say it now you're married."

"Convenience only."

"Nevertheless." She took a sip. "You know my rules."

"Ah, you're a cruel mistress. Not even a kiss for old time's sake?"

"Kiss your wife, Barnaby—you won't succeed with me." Raising her glass, she moved past him and cast her gaze about the room. There were almost four hundred people in attendance; it was deeply unlikely she would see George Comerford, and she could easily keep her distance from him. There was no reason for her to think about the sight of his curly head between her legs, or the gruff note in his voice as he whispered praise against the skin of her thigh.

No reason at all.

Goodness, it was warm in here. She snapped out her fan and fanned her chest. No more thoughts of George. Tonight, she would find herself another lover and all would be well.

One thing was for certain: she could not afford to leave it much longer.

Chapter Two

George was bored. Although he would rather have chopped off his thumb than admit it to the world, he would rather be at home in his library with a novel. One of those sensationalist gothic ones. Or perhaps a romance. Some poetry.

He had ascertained within five minutes that in Miss Stanley's eyes, his only charm was his wealth and title. Admittedly, most young ladies were interested in these, but he had some ridiculous notion of his future wife enjoying his company, too.

He was, he could freely admit, an optimist.

"Mr Comerford?" she asked. He looked down into her cherubic face, realising by her note of irritation that this must not have been the first time she'd said his name.

"Ah, I'm sorry." He offered her a charming smile. "I must have been lost in my thoughts."

"I asked if you would ask me to dance."

Across the room, George spied a familiar head of blonde curls.

How he knew it was hers, he was not entirely sure. Perhaps it was the angle at which she held her head, the way the curls fell across her neck. Or perhaps it was the colour of them, burnished gold by candlelight; flaxen by the light of the sun.

Or perhaps it was the voluptuous curves that accompanied the hair. The generous swell of breasts he had pressed his face into, a rounded waist he delighted in, and hips that he had gripped as he'd held her against him.

Although she was clothed now, gowned in a dress of elegant red, he knew what every inch of her naked body looked like. The curves, the lines, the soft rolls he had kissed with a poet's adoration.

This was, naturally, not the first time he had seen her since their parting, but he was still swamped by restless need. The urge to prowl to her side and command her hand in the next dance would do him no favours. Besides, it would ruin the languid, unbothered reputation he had been at such pains to establish. George Comerford did not pursue ladies with such single-mindedness.

Even so, he disliked that she was there flirting with other gentlemen. A wave of something alarmingly possessive rose in him, and he turned back to his wearying partner.

"A dance," he said, with a flourishing bow. "Would you be so good as to grant me the waltz, Miss Stanley?"

She made what he was certain was a valiant effort to blush, and he almost applauded the attempt. Despite her distinct lack of interest in *him*, she was evidently prepared to do anything in order to secure his viscountcy and fortune.

"I've heard you like to write poetry," she said as they took their places in the middle of the ballroom, her hand resting lightly on his.

Another half an hour before he could escape her.

"I do," he said.

"Like Byron."

No one would ever quite be like Byron, either with his sudden rise to popularity or the subsequent scandals with the now-infamous Caroline Lamb. The comparison was at once flattering and dire. "Somewhat," he said.

"I thought you might like to write *me* some." She fluttered her lashes.

He was temporarily speechless. "Is that so?"

"Well I *am* extraordinarily pretty. Quite a few gentlemen have been obliging enough to say that if they had the power, they would write a sonnet to the brilliance of my eyes." If she possessed any subtlety, she was not using it on him. "Do you not agree, sir?"

He could not help thinking again of Caroline, who had never once demanded anything other than honesty from him. She would have abhorred the idea of false flattery. "Why, it means nothing at all if it is not from the heart, darling," she had said to him on more than one occasion.

There was no denying she was aware of her charms, but at least she wielded them with a lighter hand than Miss Stanley.

"I'm afraid," he said absently, "I am not much in the habit of writing poetry for young ladies."

Save, of course, a certain lady who was not in the heart of her youth.

Deciding another half hour with a young lady interested in nothing but his fortune would be intolerable, he guided her from the dance, encountering a fearsome little scowl that almost made him laugh.

Fortune hunters could take their shot at him; they would always miss.

"Ah," he said, spying his friend. "Hawkridge."

James Hawkridge had been a friend of his since his Cambridge days, and although he was not titled, he owned a tidy estate in Cornwall. Hopefully it would be good enough to please Miss Stanley.

"Comerford," Hawkridge said with a start. "What are you doing here?"

"It's been an age since we last met."

Hawkridge's only sign of confusion was a slow blink—he had seen George just two days ago at White's. "Yes."

"Allow me to present Miss Stanley to you. Miss Stanley, this is my very good friend, Mr James Hawkridge." He placed her hand on Hawkridge's arm, and could almost see the way she assessed his friend, calculating the approximate worth of his property and determining if she was worth his attention. By her eventual smile, she evidently decided he was.

Excellent.

"Delighted to make your acquaintance," Hawkridge said, after a searching glance at George to clarify his intentions. "Don't suppose you would do me the honour of dancing?"

Miss Stanley sent George a particularly poisonous look he supposed he deserved. "I should be delighted to dance the remainder of the waltz with you."

George gestured them extravagantly past him and abandoned the dance in search of refreshments. There was, at least, wine, and he poured himself a generous glass before leaning against a pillar in order to watch the proceedings. James was flirting extravagantly, and Miss Stanley was encouraging him at every juncture. Caroline was nowhere to be seen.

Irritated with himself for caring when she had insisted on ending things between them, he abandoned his pillar and made his way to the card room. When he got there, however, he near collided with a figure just leaving it.

And, curse his luck, out of all four hundred guests, it had to be Caroline Spenser herself.

Caroline stopped short at the sight of George so close to her—closer than he had been since the day they had left Worthington Hall. All evening, she had been flirting, hoping she might feel something with at least one potential patron. But now, pinned like a butterfly underneath the weight of his gaze, all the desire she had been waiting to feel came rushing through.

And it was with a man who would be married imminently.

A man to whom she had become altogether too close to in the past. Worthington Hall had been a wash of madness, a desire too deep to deny, but more than that, it had been an exercise in intimacy. Lying awake in the early hours of the morning, the sensation of his fingers threading through her hair. Gentle kisses after he had finished with her.

It was the first time in a long time that she had allowed herself to be held, and it had been intoxicating. That was why she had cut him off before she could risk getting attached.

And now here he was, a manifestation of her desires, his eyes darkening the longer he looked at her.

"Caroline." His voice was low, a little rough.

She couldn't let him know how much he affected her. "Mr Comerford," she said, batting her eyelashes like she might at any gentleman who greeted her. "Where is the delightful Miss Stanley?"

"Securing a fortune for herself elsewhere." His gaze travelled down her body, and she fought the urge to preen. "That gown is divine, Caroline. You are divine in it."

"Thank you, darling." She stepped aside and gestured him in the card room, where she had been making the rounds. Gentlemen who enjoyed cards were often tempted to bet on other pleasures. "Were you heading this way? Please, don't let me stop you."

"As it happens, I was looking for some air." He offered her his arm. "Will you accompany me outside?"

She bit her lip, hesitating. "I shouldn't."

"But you want to."

"But I want to," she conceded, and accepted his arm. He guided her to the French doors thrown open to welcome in the cool night breeze. The billowing curtains brushed the bare skin at the top of her arms, and as she stepped onto the balcony, she looked down on the onto the street. She felt like a naive girl on her first assignation.

Ridiculous.

Rather thrilling.

She was not in the market for any more scandal than her usual variety, but this *was* fun. The push and pull, the forbidden nature of it. The desire.

In the darkness, he was almost more compelling than in the light, though only because she had his features memorised. A certain silver in his brown eyes. The roguish slant of his smile. Not quite a smirk—he was not a rake—but something approaching one.

"Caroline," he said, his voice low and caressing. The sound of it was delicious against her flushed skin. He took her wrist now, thumb smoothing across the soft material of her gloves.

"We said we would not act as lovers here," she said, though she had been the one to dictate the terms.

"I know."

"So we shouldn't."

"I agree." His hand touched her elbow, at the precise place her gloves ended. His fingers were bare, and heat swelled through her. Her nipples hardened. "It would be foolish. And in full view of the ballroom." He tilted his head, and a slow smile dawned across his face. His eyes glittered in the dim light. "Although perhaps you like that."

"Perhaps."

"A thrill. The potential of discovery." His hand travelled up her arm to the puff of her sleeves. Then down, caressing her breast. The heavy ache of it resounded through her. "I've missed these. I've missed you."

She'd missed him too. Both his conversation and the way he took control. When it came to her body, the bedchamber, she enjoyed commands, a forceful hand to bend her will. George had learnt it about her, as he had learnt so many things about her body, and she thought the domination called to him, too.

"So kiss me," she said.

He wasted no time.

His mouth was hot and demanding, capturing hers the instant she gave him leave to, and his other hand found her waist, fingers digging in through her layers to find the softness of her curves. She cupped his neck in his hands, nails biting at his skin.

Just once.

The letter in her reticule was a reminder that no matter what she wanted, she had obligations, and she must have someone to pay for them.

If only she did not crave him, and only him, so very much. Too much for it to be a mere arrangement of convenience.

The kiss was burning fire, igniting her from the inside out, and all too soon voices approached. George drew her back into the darkness, stepping away from her just enough that there was nothing immediately untoward about their appearance. If one neglected to notice, that was, precisely how out of breath they both were. Or how possessive George's hand on her wrist was, as though he sensed she was about to return to the ball.

"Not yet," he murmured.

Another couple, equally as intent on amorous activities, went by silent agreement to the other darkened corner of the balcony.

"You can hardly have me here," she said dryly. "No matter how tempting it might be."

"You would have to be quiet, certainly."

She gave him a flirtatious look and moved away. "You flatter me too much, darling. But I did not come here for you."

"No?" His voice was dark and possessive, and she loved that, too, the way it sharpened her awareness of the ache between her legs.

If he insisted, perhaps she would let him have her here, after all. The pleasure of it would be exquisite.

“You know what I am,” she said lightly. “And what I do.”

“Who are you entertaining this time?”

If only he knew. But it was better this way. “Does it matter?” She shook him free. “We agreed we would not interfere with each other once we returned to London. You have a wife to catch.” *And I cannot become attached to a man who will never be mine.*

“I am excellent at multitasking.”

She laughed. “Poor girl. You should not be so cruel.”

“When can I see you again?”

“We will attend many of the same events, no doubt.” She waved an airy hand at him, knowing that for all his possessiveness, he would not keep her against her will. “Enough, darling. Know when to let things go.”

His eyes burned into her back as she forced herself to walk away as though she felt nothing at leaving him alone on the darkened balcony.

Chapter Three

In total, including her first Season, Caroline had spent fifteen years in London. Seven of them had been during her marriage, and eight as a merry widow. Although at times she found herself under disagreeable strain, for the most part she enjoyed the life she had forged for herself.

Better she make her own way here than be beholden to a family which had near disowned her for her transgressions as a girl.

Her only concern was making the payments on Jacqueline's dowry. Without a lover to boost her meagre income, she was at risk of not being able to pay it at all, and she couldn't have that.

"You're scowling," Sir Percy Somerville, her long-time friend, said as she walked into her drawing room to greet him. "And yet still look remarkably lovely."

"Of course I do, darling." She presented her cheek for him to kiss, and he did so with an amused expression she did not appreciate. Perhaps surprisingly, she had Sir Percy had never been lovers, although they had known each other since her marriage. Then, he had been young and foolish, enjoying all London had to offer. Now he was older, madly in love with his estranged wife, and, in her opinion, as foolish as ever.

"Thank you for agreeing to join me tonight," he said. "I'm sure you have far better things to be doing."

Silently, Caroline cursed her generous heart. Instead of embarking on more profitable endeavours, she was participating in a scheme that would likely hurt everyone involved. "Not at all," she said throatily, deciding to make the most of it. "You know I delight in scandal."

"I do." His voice was dry. "Even so, let me give you a small token of appreciation." From his pocket, he withdrew a diamond bracelet, fastening it about her wrist despite her protests. "Sell it after tonight."

Of all her acquaintances, Sir Percy was the only one to know about the money she sent to the country—and why. Perhaps she should have demurred, but she merely held it to the light. "A pretty trinket."

"Don't accept a penny less than five hundred."

"And generous, too." Her earlier reservations eased, and she gave him a winning smile. Five hundred pounds did not a generous dowry make, and she needed to commission new gowns for the remainder of the Season, but it was a start. "You have my gratitude."

"Not at all." Sir Percy held out his arm. "Shall we? The opera awaits, my lady."

The night was warm, heralding summer, and she toyed with the edge of her wrap as she followed him out to his waiting carriage. For all they had been friends these past fifteen years, his relationship with his wife was a mystery that confounded Caroline.

Sir Percy had been the one to pursue her; she was almost twenty years his junior and had not wished to be married. Her mother insisted, however, and married they were. Deluded, perhaps, by the force of his affection, he had believed his love would bring her around to loving him in return, but she had never been anything but cold towards him. Now, rumour had it that she had another lover. And so, instead of confronting her about it, Sir Percy had retaliated by enlisting her to make the girl jealous.

A fool.

But a kind one, a generous one, and one Caroline deeply wished to see happy.

"We might be late," he said, checking his pocket watch. "I'd hoped to be established for when she arrives."

"Nonsense," she said, taking a hand to her curls and mussing them somewhat. "If we arrive late, she will only assume it's because you rose from my bed too late."

"*If* she notices once the curtain is up."

"A lady always notices when her husband is accompanying another woman to the opera."

"Even when she is herself accompanied by a dashing young man?"

"You are perfectly dashing," she said firmly. "And I am positively notorious. The combination will not escape her,

I assure you." Ladies such as Lady Cecily Somerville always sought the company of the most fashionable young gentleman. Caroline knew—she had once been just like her. But no matter how difficult their home life, she strongly believed that even a young wife could not be blind to Sir Percy's handsomeness. In his early forties, he was perhaps a little greying around the ears, but nature had blessed him with charm and an excellent figure.

There was a time when Caroline might have been tempted to make a move. But disastrously in love as he was, he had eyes for no one but the flame-haired beauty he had married.

And now, the temptation had escaped her too, replaced by a frustratingly handsome man who had pinned her against the wall and recited poetry in her ear as he sank into her.

At the thought, her stomach tightened.

Really, it was his fault that she had not found another lover; what other gentleman could live up to the erotic imagery that George Comerford had left behind like a flare of light against closed eyelids? He was a firework in the dark—no candle could compare.

At least Sir Percy would expect nothing from her but light, meaningless flirtation.

He did not have one of the upper tier boxes in the opera, but they were nevertheless high enough to watch the glittering of the enormous chandelier. Candlelight reflected off the gilding in a way that seemed almost magical; for a moment, she was young again, the glamour of the city easing her heartbreak.

Sir Percy leant in, his mouth brushing the shell of her ear. "Do you see her?"

"Of course." Cecily was sitting in the box almost directly opposite, her red hair catching in the light. Much as she was sympathetic to Sir Percy's plight, Caroline felt a little for the beautiful young woman who had been so adamant against accepting her husband's proposal. It was no fun thing to be forced into marriage.

Sir Percy had been smitten enough to think that his love would be enough. Caroline could have told him otherwise.

"She's watching us," Caroline said, leaning in, her breasts brushing his arm. "And no doubt she assumes the worst."

"Good." There was no satisfaction in his voice, merely grim pain. "Perhaps when she comes home tonight, she might speak to me."

Caroline tilted her head, ringlets brushing the bare skin of her neck as she considered him. "And you believe this is truly the best way to win her back?"

"I've tried reasoning with her to no avail. What else am I supposed to do?"

Caroline looked at the young lady in the other box. They were too far apart to make out much other than the fiery hair, but she suspected there was a mulish cast to her jaw. "You could be patient and give her space."

"And watch her flaunt her beaus across London?"

She looked at him pointedly, and he gave a wry, crooked smile. "Yes, I'm aware I'm doing precisely the same thing."

"Well, we are making her jealous, at least." She gave him an adoring smile, but before she could see what effect that might have had, her gaze snagged on a gentleman standing in the pit and staring at her.

Ordinarily, that was where she would be: in the pit with all the other gentlemen and ladies of the *ton* who did not have a box for the Season. That was, if she attended the opera alone at all, which was rare.

But Comerford, she knew, *had* purchased a box for the Season, so she could think of no reason he would not be in it.

There was a young lady by his side, a dark-haired beauty who had bewitched many of the Season's bachelors. She was pixie-thin, and her neckline daringly low. Some gentlemen preferred waifs they could easily pick up, whose stomachs were flat, whose thighs were slim and easily spread.

George Comerford, who had explored every inch of Caroline's body with his tongue, did not.

He still had not looked away. There was the darkness of possession in his gaze. The low throb of jealousy.

She was immediately back in the library at Worthington House, her front pressed against the books, his hand at her neck, and his mouth whispering filthy secrets into her ear. The way he'd held her against him had made her toes curl.

"We should be sensible about this," she'd told him as they'd dressed after a late-night rendezvous.

"In what way?"

"When we return to London."

"Oh?"

She'd kept her voice light as she'd looked at him, biting her lip in a way she knew he found irresistible. He'd said so against her stomach, murmuring his appreciation into the soft rise and fall of her flesh. "You are on the hunt for a wife."

"So?"

"So it would do you no good to be seen in my company."

His smile was especially roguish, and reminded her a little of Byron when he had been the height of fashion. "The purpose of being in your company, my dear, is not to be seen."

"Yes," she said wryly. "But word gets out. And I am not what one might consider reputable."

He kissed her neck, interrupting her as she laced up her stays. "Why, what is your reputation?"

"You know very well."

"I know that you have had your fair share of lovers," he mused, teeth grazing the tender skin below her ears. "And I know I am fortunate enough to benefit from your experience."

"Yes, but, George." She twisted in his arms so he would meet her gaze. "We both know that you have worked long and hard to establish yourself, and you are under obligation to marry. You admitted as much to me yourself. I will not get in the way of that."

He pulled back, and she wondered if he saw her excuse for what it was: a reason not to allow herself to become too invested. He was to marry, and she could not lose her head or her heart again. Her arguments over his reputation were flimsy, and they both knew it.

Still, there was resignation in his eyes, and she knew she had won. "Then let us waste no time," he said, and he had undone all her work in dressing.

Now he was watching her with something hard and fixed in his expression. The sort of expression she might have seen in a vengeful Greek statue, all marble and hard, uncompromising features.

How odd that she had once thought him soft.

He finally looked away and tossed a comment to Miss Browning, who laughed, showing perfect white teeth. They were too far away for Caroline to hear the sound, but she knew it would be softly tinkling. A girl like that never laughed with her belly.

Once, Caroline had been taught to be that way, too.

"Do you know that gentleman?" Sir Percy asked, nodding at Comerford. She could feel her heartbeat in her ears, and she cursed George Comerford from the bottom of her heart.

"Somewhat," she said.

"A past lover?"

"Yes. He is looking for a wife now."

Sir Percy gave her a sympathetic look. "And you do not consider yourself a candidate for his hand?"

"I consider myself a candidate for no man's hand," she told him, prodding him in the arm with her fan. If Comerford was looking, she could not see him. "I would not make a proper wife."

"Even if a gentleman wishes to marry you?"

"You are mistaken," she said, turning to the curtains as they jerked and slid away to the side, revealing the stage. "It is not marriage George Comerford wants from me."

Chapter Four

As George lay with Caroline's head on his heart, he listened to the sound of her breathing, the flow of it soft against his skin. It struck him as a particular kind of privilege to see her in these rare, unguarded moments. When she was in his arms in this way, she was nothing more than Caroline Spenser, and he was nothing more than George Comerford, and they were nothing more than the sum of their time together.

"In passion's embrace, all boundaries fade," he said against the silk of her hair. "As souls entwine beneath the starry glade, No earthly tether can restrain its flight, For passion knows no bounds, no end in sight."

She stirred sleepily, and he felt her cheek curve against him. "Where did you read that?"

"Now that would be telling." He ran his fingers down her plump arm, tossed carelessly over his chest. The week had progressed from clandestine, frantic, desperate couplings to

this—something frighteningly close to intimacy. "Do you like to read?"

"The only poetry I read is the kind ladies should never consume," she said, and he laughed.

"Is that where you learnt all your tricks?"

"No," she said, and twisted like a cat, her breasts pressing against his chest as she shifted to look up at him, the beginnings of a wicked, knowing smile on her mouth. "I learnt my tricks from a gentleman who frequented brothels a great deal before frequenting me. That was early in my career as a mistress."

"I should thank him."

"Oh, I have no idea where he is now," she said carelessly. "I never keep track of my former lovers."

"Am I to take it you won't keep track of me once we part?"

The smile slipped from her lips, and he regretted the question almost immediately. "When we part," she said, walking her fingers up his chest, "it shall be as though we never met."

Well, she was certainly behaving as though they'd never met.

He had never ascertained why she had refused to continue their relationship after Worthington Hall, but he had told himself he accepted her decision—until he saw her on the arm of another gentleman. Heat flooded him at the way Sir Percy Somerville put his hand on hers, commanding her attention with the ease of someone who knew her well. She had often been seen with him—gossip spread in London like wildfire—but he'd thought their time together had ended with Somerville's marriage.

Evidently not.

Why had she decided that Somerville was a better fit for her purpose than him? Yes, he was to be married soon, but he had thought she didn't consort with married men, and Sir Percy was certainly married.

Jealousy prickled across his skin. If their time in Worthington Hall had been any less to both their liking, he would have assumed he did not match up to her expectations. But she had shown every sign of enjoying herself. And the fact she had tossed him aside and taken up with another gentleman instead rankled.

She was not his, but by God he wanted her to be.

The thing that consumed him was not the pleasure, although he still dreamt about her curves. It was the time after, in those quiet moments between sleep. Intimacy that had him writing verse in her name and spending days wondering about the precise shade of her eyes. He still didn't think he had a word for it, and wasn't that a travesty, that nothing in the human language could adequately capture their knowing sparkle?

Yet she was now entertaining other gentlemen as she had entertained him. Falling asleep with Sir Percy in her bed and waking to his slow, ardent kisses.

The feeling inside him rose until it burned.

The first half of the opera was indeterminable. A dragging of time that seemed to last forever and yet went by in a flash of longing.

When at last the curtains closed for the intermission, Miss Browning glanced over her shoulder. As the youngest daughter of a viscount and one of the most highly sought-after ladies of the Season, she knew precisely what she was about. The only reason she had accompanied him tonight was to make her other beaus—an earl and a disastrously rich gentleman with land in Derbyshire—jealous.

From what George knew of her, she would choose the Earl.

"Lord Darlington is on his way," she said, proving him right. "Make a show of having enjoyed your time with me, then relinquish me to him." Her gaze slid meaningfully to Caroline's box.

He could hardly argue with that, just as he could hardly argue with not being the prize she wished to hook. Better they were both upfront and honest with one another.

"I wish you luck," he said, before the Earl was upon them.

After a moment of feigning interest in Miss Browning, he bowed to her request for refreshment, and left. From there, he walked the gilded corridors until finally he saw Caroline on her escort's arm. As though compelled, her gaze slid to his, and hunger flashed across her eyes before she looked away. For all she had cultivated city polish—as he had, after leaving Cambridge—there was no doubting that she knew what it was to want.

"Excuse me," he heard her say to Somerville, and then she was approaching him, steps light and her brow raised. "Did you truly come to seek me out?"

"Is that what you think?"

"I think yes."

"I came for ratafia." He reached past her to take a glass. "For Miss Browning."

That was worth it to see the irritation spark in her eyes. "Is that so?" she asked. "Then forgive me for intruding."

He took the glass and held it loosely in one hand, keeping his gaze fixed rigidly on her. "Does he please you more than me?"

"Somerville?" Her laugh scraped lower, and his need for her ballooned. "Why do you ask?"

He would have her. He was a man consumed.

"Make your excuses," he said, and handed her the glass. "When the curtains rise, I'll be waiting for you."

"What makes you think I will come?" Her voice was throaty; her eyes were bright.

"Because I have bid it." He withdrew, the glass in his hand. "And because you enjoy it when I make demands of you."

"Is that so?" she murmured. Her irises were azure, no longer grey but utterly blue. Jewels, precious beyond measure. "What of the lovely Miss Browning?"

"She has as much interest in me as I do in her."

"Oh, so she is not to be your next wife?"

"No."

"A shame your outing here was for nothing."

He could not help his smile as he raised the glass to her in a toast. "It was not for nothing."

#

"I don't think I have ever seen you look so pleased with yourself," Sir Percy said as she returned to his side.

Caroline clucked her tongue, though there was an unfamiliar pit of excitement in her stomach. "Nonsense."

"Is that so." His voice was dry. "Let us both leave after the interval, if you are intending to abandon me in my box. I had rather not have my wife see another lady leave me."

"Darling," she said as they entered the box. "I would never be so cruel."

"Are you about to do something foolish?"

Yes.

Her affairs were, on occasion, fun. Even if the gentlemen in question were bores, she often could coax them into pleasing her in bed.

But George was not a bore, and although he was eager to learn, he needed very little coaxing. In an alarming turn of events, she found she enjoyed conversation with him.

Horrifying. Distressing.

Oddly addictive.

"I always do foolish things," she said. "But would you rather I stayed?"

Sir Percy shook his head. "No. Enjoy your time with your young lover; I will retire to bed. Will you have a means of getting home?"

George would likely take her home himself. Or she would find another method of leaving. "I expect so."

"Try not to be *too* foolish, my dear," he said, patting her hand with a fondness that verged on exasperation.

Understandable.

Usually, she had a mode of conduct that she adhered to. Although she was known for her many affairs, she did not behave like a bawdy whore in public places.

After all, part of her reputation—and the reason most hostesses still invited her, although Almack's was beyond her reach—was that she knew how to be discreet. And yet here she was, considering an assignation in the opera house of all places. How positively . . .

Delicious.

As the curtain rose, Caroline looked at Cecily, who was flirting extravagantly with her nervous escort. Then she glanced back at Sir Percy's tight expression.

What a pair of peacocks.

"I shall offer you this advice just once," she said, rising to her feet and commanding, with a slight touch to his arm, that he do the same. "And I say it with love in my heart, because I wish you happy."

"This doesn't bode well," he said wryly, finally looking away from the lady who had unwittingly stolen his heart.

"Stop playing games. She may never have understood your affection, and she certainly made it clear she did not want it when you offered. That was your folly—the best thing you can do for her now is to treat her with respect. Flaunting your supposed mistress in front of her will likely make her jealous, and it is certainly apt revenge for the crimes she has committed against you, but marriage is not war, and if it is, then you should not play your battle from a position of weakness."

"Love is not weakness," he said, brackets forming on either side of his mouth.

She raised a shoulder. "As you say. But you are handing her the bullets and letting her fire the pistol, and wondering why it is that you are the only one to bleed."

"Tonight, I fired the pistol."

"And does this feel like a victory?"

At the flicker of pain in his eyes, she relented, leaning up to kiss his cheek. "Try seducing her, my darling. You never know—you may find that yields better results than actions designed to increase her resentment. And you have the benefit of experience behind you. I'll wager you know more about pleasing a woman than that boy she's currently entertaining. Use that advantage."

He looked at her with an expression caught between respect and fear. "You are a holy terror."

"Thank you."

"It was not entirely a compliment," he murmured, but his lips twitched as they left the box. "Be careful with that boy of yours."

"He's not a boy."

"Passion like that can destroy a man. Believe me when I say I know."

She removed her hand from his arm. "Go home, Percy. Talk to your wife and leave me to my affairs." The bracelet slid down her arm as she raised her hand in farewell. "Good luck."

He nodded and strode in the opposite direction. Caroline watched him go for a few moments before turning and making her way along the deserted hallways that encircled the pit. The lamps cast a flickering, golden light across the opulence, and the carpet was thick underfoot, muffling her steps.

She had not gone far before a man emerged from the gloom of a box entry, his silhouette splitting from the shadows. George, fair hair brushed back, eyes sparking at the sight of her. She already knew she was making a mistake, but he was a light to her fuse, and she had handed him the matches.

There was nothing else for her to do tonight but let them burn.

"Come," was all he said as, a hand on her back, he led her to an empty antechamber. She was not an unmarried maiden; she knew precisely what would happen when the door closed behind her, and yet when George spun her around so her back was against the wood, his face a mask of shadows, she had to bite back a gasp.

"You must be quiet," he murmured. "Lest we are discovered."

"I know how to avoid discovery."

"Ah yes. I remember." His mouth descended on hers now for a blazing kiss, and she returned in kind, sliding a hand underneath his coat to his waistcoat then undoing his buttons.

Somewhere, distantly, a soprano hit an eye-watering note, and it resonated through her like a tolled bell.

"I don't like seeing you with other gentlemen," he said in a low, possessive voice. His teeth caught her lobe, not gently, and she bit her lip. "I especially don't like watching them touch you."

"You do not own me," she said, tipping her chin back.

"No? But I want to." He palmed her breast and made a pleased noise at the back of his throat. "I want to be the only man permitted to touch you here." There was a savage, primal light in his eyes, and all the words she had been meaning to say—about how he had no right to claim on her—died on her lips.

This, she liked.

This she liked very much indeed.

He ran both hands around her waist and down to her backside, squeezing her and pressing her against his erection. "It drove me half mad to watch you up there with him."

"If this is half mad, then I would gladly do it again."

"No." With one hand, he pushed up her skirts; with his other, he slid two fingers between her thighs. Her eyes closed in relief. How long had it been since someone had touched her there? Weeks—since she had returned to London from Worthington Hall at the end of April. Five weeks at least. Maybe longer. "I don't want you to see him again. Do you understand me?"

"This was not the plan," she managed.

"The plan? Do you think I planned this?" He caught the nape of her neck in his hand and dragged her in for another rough kiss. His other hand worked between her legs, plunging inside her with a roughness that only added to her pleasure. "When you ended things between us, I hadn't intended to think about you again after we parted."

"But you do?"

"I wanted to take you on the balcony at Lady Peterborough's ball," he told her, and she squirmed, breathless and wanting. "I wanted to push you against the wall and hold a hand over your mouth to stop you whimpering as I made a mess of you in front of all the other guests."

She clenched helplessly around him. "I would have let you."

"I know."

"I didn't deny you because I had no desire to—" She could not think with his finger crooking inside her, finding the place that brought about her peak the fastest. "You are to be married."

"I am not yet."

There was also the matter of payment; she had given him her favours for free, because she had wanted to, because she had liked him. But if he was insisting on being her only lover, and if she accepted, then she would need more from him.

It galled her to admit it.

"Did he expect to go home with you tonight?" he demanded.

"No."

"Good." That single word was vicious, and he pressed the head of his cock against her slickness. "I am not even close to being done with you."

The audacity of the statement thrilled her, although she did her best not to show it. "And if I am done with you?"

He took the crook of her knee, lifting it to one side as he pushed himself inside her. She made a muted sound of satisfaction. That was always how it had been between them.

"Quiet, love," he said, one hand across her mouth. Then he leant in closer. "Liar. If that were true, you would not be here."

True, she could not deny it. Just a few walls away, the *ton* were gathered to listen to an opera, and if she made too much noise, they would inevitably risk discovery and ruin. Many things could be forgiven behind closed doors, but this was sordid, even for her.

He was right: she did delight in it.

When they both found completion, he would be gentle again, tender, but until then, he gave her this, and it was what she needed. The streak of cruelty that always heated her blood and made her hate him, just a little.

Everything was so much heightened when there was an edge of pain to the pleasure.

"Look at me, Caro."

She turned her gaze to his face, watching the hazy movement of pleasure across it.

"That's right," he crooned, his palm still over her mouth, her gasps and cries stifled. His breath was short, choppy. "Keep your eyes on me."

They were still fully clothed, her skirts bunching between them. The door behind her rattled, and he rested his elbow against it. His breath was hot on her cheek. They were bathed in darkness.

"I want to be the only man you take as a lover," he said as he thrust into her again. "No one else."

The proprietorial nature of his demand added to the heat inside her. Time and time again, she had reminded herself that it was dangerous to grow attached, especially to a man on the hunt for a wife, but it was as though she had spent the last five weeks underwater and now she could at last breathe again.

There was just one last thing to settle.

"I am expensive to keep," she said.

Surprise flashed in his eyes, there and gone again, and she wondered if this was an insult he would not bear. But his teeth closed around her ear, and the flash of pain shuddered through her like a climax. "Name your price," he said against her neck, and moved to sink his teeth into her shoulder. She thought distantly she would have to cover the marks until they faded. "I'm a rich man."

Oh she was playing with fire. But she did so like the way it crisped her skin.

His hands sank into the softness of her waist, and he made another gruff noise of appreciation. "Tell me you accept. Be mine, Caroline. Only mine."

She was too practical a woman to be taken in merely by the hoarse note in a man's voice as he neared release. Or even the feel of him inside her, guiding her closer to her own peak. But then his thumb found the sensitive nub between her slick folds, and she exhaled sharply. This was cheating, playing her body like a harp, as though he were a master plucking her every string and compelling her every pleasure. Drugged, dazed, lost to the feel of his hands and his mouth and his body, she struggled to hold on to her last modicum of reason.

"Tell me." His other hand closed around her throat, just hard enough that she could feel the blood pound and the scrape of air. Her climax loomed, alarmingly close. "Tell me you will not take another man to be your lover so long as I am."

"Yes," she said as she tipped over the edge. Pleasure bloomed through her and her legs trembled. "Yes."

He groaned, as though the words alone had brought him close, and he removed himself from her, turning away and spending himself in a handkerchief he had produced for the purpose.

Caroline closed her eyes and listened to the last strains of the aria, wondering how she, a woman of sense, could be about to make the same mistake for the second time in her life.

Chapter Five

Of all the places in London, Hatchards was one of George's favourites. If left to his own devices, he would spend hours there, flicking through the books and inhaling the scent of paper and fresh ink. The action calmed him, even if he merely replaced the books on the shelves and moved on. There was a difference between the crispness of newly printed books and those of his personal library, which were often far older. He prized both.

As he stepped inside, his eyes took a moment to adjust to the dim lighting. As always, it was a hub for ladies to meet, and gentlemen to meet ladies, and perhaps to buy the latest book of poetry. He sidestepped them, heading for the stairs to the second floor, which was often quieter. The wooden floorboards creaked underfoot, and he entered the first aisle, running his fingers along the embossed leather spines.

Relief spread through him, easing the tension of the past few days. Coming here, he felt like a boy discovering poetry for the first time—verse written by hot-headed men about what it meant to be alive.

It was familiar magic, and he had just opened a collection of Wordsworth's—many of the poems he already knew, but it was the action not the reveal he enjoyed—when he heard light footsteps.

He often encountered members of the *ton* here, but although he had not been granted many opportunities to hear her footsteps, he knew how she sounded.

Placing the book back on the shelf, he left his aisle and came to the mouth of another, staring at a familiar blonde head tipped towards a book in her hands. Curls fell down her neck to a thin golden necklace, and her dress was deceptively simple, a daisy-patterned muslin that might have made her look like a debutante in her first Season if he was not so familiar with the wickedness of her smile.

After their tryst the night prior, he had taken her home and she had granted him permission to see her tonight. This visit to Hatchards was a half-hearted attempt at distraction, but fate had delivered her to him on a silver platter.

"Good morning," he said as he strolled forwards. "I see I am not the only one to appreciate the finer things in life."

She snapped the book shut. "George. What are you doing here?"

"The same as you, I presume." He nodded at the book in her hand. "*To err is human, to forgive divine.*"

The challenge left her eyes, and she tilted her head, amused once again. "You know Alexander Pope?"

"Does not every man?"

"You may be surprised to hear it, but I rarely speak about literature when conversing with men."

Nor did he, but he enjoyed the way she matched him step for step, and he took up position beside her. "Naturally. What do you discuss instead? The political climate in France? The incontrovertible evidence that Wellington is the best military leader the country has seen?"

"Oh no," she said smoothly. "One must never compliment another gentleman during such times. If the man I'm with has military inclinations, I ask for his opinion on matters of war and agree with everything he says."

"How dull."

"He does not think so, I assure you."

"You should entertain more interesting men."

"You are a fool, darling, if you think I choose my lovers based on the quality of their conversation." She let the thought sit for a moment, the beginnings of a wicked smile playing around her mouth. "There are only two considerations I take into account. The size of his purse is one."

He laughed, delighting in her. "Of course. What else?"

Her lashes lowered demurely. "I could not possibly speak it aloud."

"I gather it's his size in other areas?"

"Not at all," she murmured. He caught a glimpse of the bite mark he'd left on her shoulder, and a surge of masculine satisfaction took him by surprise. "I prize generosity. After all, I have extravagant tastes."

"So you've mentioned, but I'm a very generous man."

She sashayed a little closer, still with that sinful smile on her lips. He longed to kiss it off her. "I hoped you might be."

"Minx." He adored it. "May I visit you this afternoon?"

"Did we not say tonight?"

"Let's say I'm a little eager."

"Dear me," she said, her tone teasing, "what *would* your future wife say?"

He gave her a lazy smile. "Hard to say, as we are not yet acquainted."

"Cruel man. May she break your heart."

"I rather think that unlikely." He took the book from her hands and flipped it to view the embossed cover. "Is this what you came for? Tell me and I'll buy it for you. The essays of Alexander Pope are not precisely light reading, but I'm certain you are more than capable."

"Naturally," she said, and moved past him for the stairs, where two giggling girls were climbing to the first floor, a stoic footman trailing them. "One thing you will discover about me, George, is that I am *always* more than capable." She tossed a careless smile over her shoulder. "Enjoy your perusal of the classics, Mr Comerford. I will see you tonight."

All she left behind were the essays she had been flicking through and the subtle, fragrant scent of her perfume.

It was unseemly of her to be so excited for George's arrival. Although she always enjoyed her lovers, it often felt transactional. This, however, felt like an illicit tryst, the kind that young ladies embarked on when they had been utterly seduced.

If it was his body alone, she could have tempered her anticipation. But there was more than that here: she enjoyed his mind almost as much as the time they shared. If she had not her daughter to think of, she would not have expected any return on her time.

She, too, could be generous when she had the luxury of it.

Still.

"My lady," her maid said from behind the door. "The gentleman has arrived."

Finally. As she waited for his quick step, she told her traitorous heart to calm and fluffed her hair, looking critically at her reflection. At five-and-thirty, she was no longer in her prime, but she prided herself that her looks had lasted reasonably well—better than she might have hoped at the tender age of twenty. The silken robe she wore drew attention to her breasts and the shadowed dip between them. In the flickering candlelight, the silk also caught on the rounded swell of her lower stomach, and she ran a hand across it.

When compared to the natural slimness of some of her peers, she had once been self-conscious of her plumpness. But as she had grown into a woman, she had welcomed her curves, understood what an asset they were. Now she loved every soft line of her body: her full breasts, the creases in her side, the way her stomach rolled when she bent.

How could one ever be a connoisseur of beauty and not learn to love the soft roundness of the female form?

The door opened and George stepped into her dressing room, his gaze running lazily over her figure. She met his eyes in the mirror, thoughts of her own body fading as she came to consider thoughts of his.

She smiled. "Hello, George."

"I have not stopped thinking about you since we parted," he said roughly, and it was as though his words ran fingertips along her skin. She shivered. "I think it might be madness."

"I didn't know Hatchards could inspire such passion."

He came to stand behind her, his face at the gilded top of her mirror. Both fair, his broadness perfectly matched her plumpness. The sight gratified her a tad too much, and she turned, letting her robe fall open. His gaze, predictably, travelled downwards.

"Here. I brought you something," he said, and draped a pink topaz necklace around her neck, the coolness of the metal soothing the flush that had arisen at the sight of him. "A beautiful necklace for a beautiful lady."

She reached up to touch the stones. The gold surrounding them was intricate, and glowed against her pale skin. "It's lovely."

"I hoped you'd like it."

She did—and she would have trouble letting go of this piece to sell.

Why could he not deliver entirely more standard gifts, such as diamonds or sapphires? They were beautiful, certainly, but not made and chosen to suit her colouring with such care.

"Thank you." She rose, twisting to kiss him, but he bent and scooped her into his arms. Surprised, she shrieked with laughter, but she was also a little impressed at his prowess—he was not, to her knowledge, a man who prided himself on his physicality, nor was she small in any dimension.

As she landed on the mattress, he smiled down at her. "There, that is where I would like to have you." He tugged at the belt of her robe, and it opened. He brushed the material from her breasts with quick, impatient movements, and made a sound of approval she would take to her grave. In all her years, she did not think a man had wanted her this much. "Did you know," he said kissing her shoulder, "that you have three freckles here?"

"A moment." She pushed at his chest, easing him back off her, and sat, tugging her robe back across her skin, almost shivering at the feel of it. Having him this close was an aphrodisiac all of its own, but there were certain rules she needed to establish. Boundaries she must lay—for his sake and hers.

"What?" he asked, the ardency leaving his voice. "Did I do something to upset you?"

"No, not at all." She touched the extravagant jewels at her neck. He had gone above and beyond, all because she said she had expensive tastes. Proof that he would pay whatever price necessary to have her, even if it harkened a change from their relationship in Worthington Hall.

There was no way she could make him fully understand. But she would try.

"There are just a few things we ought to establish," she said. "First."

"A few things?" He tipped her chin up so she was looking directly at him. "Then tell me. If nothing else, we are friends, are we not?"

Friends. The terrifying thing was that, unlike her other lovers, she thought she could be friends with George Comerford, and that was precisely why she must erect some boundaries between them.

"Firstly, I would like to explain why I require gifts from you."

He frowned. "Is that not the usual arrangement between a man and his mistress?"

"Yes, but I know that's not how we were in Worthington Hall."

"Ah." He drew the word out. "Is that why you ended things, because you did not want to ask for gifts?"

It was enough of the truth that she could nod.

"Foolish girl," he said, a smile quirking the corners of his lips. "You know I wouldn't have minded, so long as I could have kept you."

And what a heady, delightful prospect that was, to have been kept by him all these lonely weeks. She would have lost herself.

"That brings me to my other rules," she said.

He traced a lazy finger up the sensitive skin of her wrist. "Rules? Very well. What are they?"

"Wine," she said as she rose. "To talk about this, there must be wine."

Chapter Six

George watched as Caroline accepted the wine from the maid who brought it to the bedchamber. She tossed it back and gave him a wicked, yet not entirely steady, smile.

After their meeting in Hatchards, he had not been given reason to think anything was wrong, that he had not erred by asking too much of her. He knew she wanted him as urgently as he wanted her. But this was his first time engaging a more permanent mistress; it was entirely possible he was ignorant of some aspects of the usual arrangements.

Whatever she asked of him, he would deliver. In exchange for having her to himself, he would offer her almost everything.

"Well?" he prompted when she said nothing. "You needn't be afraid of asking things of me—you need only say the word and they are yours."

"You are all that is charming." She handed him a crystal glass filled with burgundy liquid. "But this is not about material things—this is about boundaries."

He sipped his wine, considering her carefully. There was a hectic flush to her cheeks. "Such as?"

"You may not stay the night."

"Oh?" His brows rose. At Worthington Hall, they had slept together after finishing, and he had woken to find her in his arms. The entire proceeding had felt entirely natural.

Then again, he should have known that in London, things would be different.

"At which time would you prefer me to leave?" he asked, glancing at the gilded clock on her mantelpiece.

"Whenever we have concluded the night's business." She gave him a smile. "Once we are done together, I will call for your carriage and you will go."

A shame—he had not been eager to visit her only for the pleasure her body could bring, as considerable as that was. He also prized the quieter times they were together, where lust fell into companionship. No other lady had given that to him, and been so willing to cross intellectual swords.

Still, if these were the terms he was to have her, he would obey.

"I will miss sleeping in your arms," he said simply.

She started as though his words were an unwelcome shock, and took another drink. "Well," she said. "Don't get too attached, because the moment you marry, this ends."

He had expected that, as much as he disliked the thought. "Hardly an incentive to hurry and find a wife," he said.

"But you must. You said so yourself."

"What's the rush? Afraid you'll fall in love with me?"

After a moment of stunned silence, her brow arched and she gave a low, rich chuckle. "Love? Oh no. Believe me, darling, I have no intention of falling in love."

"Then there's no need to rush. Unless you were hoping to return to another man's bed?" The thought brought another dark wave of jealousy with it, but he fought it back.

"No," she said, her voice a little rough as she came to straddle him where he sat on the edge of the bed. "There's no one else."

"Good." He was almost alarmed by the force of his response. He had wanted before, yes, but never with this single-minded ferocity. "Now, what if I wish to take you out and have you on my arm?"

"You'd better not."

"Why?"

Her mouth ghosted along his jaw. "My reputation is *extremely* poor."

"Because you take lovers?"

"Precisely. Mothers despise me and seek to keep their daughters far away from my corruption." She gave a humourless laugh. "You would do well not to flaunt me across London if you are in search of a wife."

He had never been less inclined to marry. "I hardly think my reputation will suffer." He unpinned her hair, letting it fall in glorious curls across her shoulders. "*Even* if I should take a lover."

"Can you be so certain?"

"It's not so unusual for a gentleman to take a mistress, Caroline."

She stiffened above him. "Perhaps you are right. Perhaps it matters little whether you are seen to take me as a lover. But you know the thing that galls me—the thing that has always galled me—is the self-serving way gentlemen condemn women and yet are so forgiving of their own. A man may have several lovers and his reputation remains intact. But a lady—give me a lady who conducts affairs openly across London who does not have doors closed in her face." Her grey eyes flashed with anger. "The law strips women of autonomy; either they belong to their fathers or their husbands, and woe betide them if they fall foul of another man's greed. Yet if a man were in that position, ruled by his wife, you think him pitiful." Her mouth tightened, and he could feel her rage as though it burned from under her skin. "And if a woman has the misfortune to fall prey to a man who cares nothing for the moral laws to which we have all been subjected, she is the one who must face censure."

George brushed the hair back from her face. "Like you?" he asked softly.

"Oh, as for me—perhaps I deserve it. Heaven knows I have not behaved as a well-bred lady over the years. But there are other women, better than I, whose reputations have suffered."

"I doubt they are better than you," he said, running his hands from her hips to her shoulders. "But I concede your points. We men are hypocrites. My question is merely this: if you are so certain of the problem, what is your solution?"

Her brow rose. "Can one not witness inequality without having a path forward?"

"What is the point of one without the other?"

"We may not all have the strength of mind to propose an active solution, but we may all feel the effects of injustice."

"Ah, perhaps," he said, enjoying the challenge, the way she refused to back down. "If you did not have the strength of mind to articulate your argument with such eloquence, I would not think you capable of a solution. But I have been impressed with the surest certainty of both your force of mind and your intelligence."

Her arms slid around his neck. "I'm afraid my solution might shock you."

"I'm considered by many to be liberal-minded."

"Then shall we test that theory?" She leant in, hot breath against his cheek. "Equality in the eyes of the law; permission for the eldest daughter to inherit ahead of a younger son. The right for women to steer our country just as men do. Fairness in reproach. If one sex must endure the burden of criticism, then so must the other. If a lady is condemned for seeking a lover outside marriage, then so must a gentleman. And conversely, if a gentleman is not criticised for keeping mistresses, then neither must mistresses be judged for being kept." Her nose brushed against his. "Is that not shocking?"

"Only if one believes women to be inferior."

"Am I to believe you are that forward thinking?"

"Women are different," he said, trying to sort through his thoughts as she divested herself of her robe. "And they have different roles. Men cannot bear children."

"They take part in their creation." Her voice was bitter as she leant back. "And they are at liberty to abandon their offspring without any repercussions."

"That, I would argue, is not always true." He slid his fingers into the glossy weight of her hair. "If I were to have a bastard, I would provide for them. And any man who does not is judged accordingly."

"Yes, but is he ruined?" There was a note he didn't recognise in her voice. Anger, though not directed at him. "Is he thrust into marriage with the next available girl so his reputation is not wholly lost?"

Frowning, he looked at her carefully. "Is there something you wish to tell me?"

"Nothing." She kissed him then, hard on the mouth, tasting of wine. "Enough talking."

His body was more than willing to obey, but although she was hungry for him, and he for her, part of his mind was still occupied with what she had let slip.

Her anger. Her resentment. He knew little of her former marriage save that it had been to a much older gentleman—perhaps forty years her senior—and he had died, as such men were wont to do. But perhaps he should have known more about it, and what reason she had for such bitterness.

When they were done and she lay in the crook of his arm, spent and tired, her eyes closed and her breath soft, he wondered how he might compel her to open up to him. He had not known until now, watching her speak with such passion, how important it was to know all her angles and corners. Every hidden part.

Unpleasantness was not something he usually courted, but he had the nameless urge to uncover all the unpleasantness she had endured and air it, cast light on it, let it heal.

If this was nothing but desire, it was more than he had ever bargained for.

Caroline woke in the early hours of the morning, her bare body still cradled against George's, and she sat up, looking at him through the strains of dawn light. Summer had brought with it merry birds and burning sun, and Caroline felt the pressure of it tighten her throat.

She should not have slept beside him. That was the wine's fault—there was no other explanation. Certainly not the grave way he had looked at her as he had listened to her anger and not judged her for it. Not the way he had made love to her—for it could not be termed anything different, even with his hand to her throat—and held her in the spluttering candlelight, terribly familiar, wonderfully safe.

That ought to have been when she'd broken free and called for the carriage. Instead, she had let herself be lulled into sleep, more peaceful than she had known it to be for a long time.

Perhaps even since Worthington Hall.

She always enjoyed her lovers, and took pleasure from them as selfishly as they took pleasure from her, but none had made her feel safe the way George did—as though she truly could make any demands of him, and he would see them through.

But she could not allow him to remain until full morning, coming down to breakfast as though they shared a life.

They would share a bed, nothing more.

The sooner he married, the better for her fickle heart.

"George," she said, and moved the blankets from him. "Wake up."

He stirred sleepily, slitting open one eye. "What is it?"

"You must leave."

"Now?"

"Yes."

"It's very early." The eye closed again. "A few more minutes, love, and I shall be ready for you."

"I will call for your carriage." She swung her feet out of bed, but he caught at her wrist, halting her progress.

"Wait." His hair was tousled in the dawn light, his chest bare and lightly scattered with soft blonde hair. She had run her fingers through it the previous night as he had thrust into her, and she was dismayed to find she could still feel the sensation as though it had been seconds, not hours, ago.

"What for?"

"You are overly hasty." He dragged her hand back to his mouth and slowly sat up, stretching and rolling out his shoulders. "Come here and let me greet you properly."

It was altogether too easy to acquiesce to his demands, to let the command in his voice rule her body. He hauled her closer, rolling her on to her back and pinning her wrists against the bed. Just tightly enough she could feel the blood throb in her fingers. She softened under him.

"Better," he said, the sleepiness in his eyes replaced by something entirely more raw. He bit her lip, giving it a sharp tug she felt down to her core. "If I must leave, at least let me take something to remember you by."

Her back arched as he kissed between her breasts, and although she knew she had but to say a word and he would stop, she found she no longer wanted to.

After, she would insist he leave.

He pushed inside her with a groan, already hard and she wet and willing, and his eyes glazed. A distant part of her thought she could bear to see him above her like this, commanding yet vulnerable, utterly hers, for a good while longer.

An alarming thought, but it took root in her chest, winding around such vital things as her heart and lungs.

His hand came to her throat, and it was lightning in her veins, her body tightening around him in helpless, exquisite pleasure. In her experience, the things that were the most wrong were often the most right, and although she knew she ought to run from him—from this—she could not quite bear for it to end.

She held on until the very last moment before oblivion took her.

It was many more hours before she called for his carriage.

Chapter Seven

The days slipped by like jewels, each one a little brighter than the next. George continued to see her in secret, arriving at her house to dine, or sometimes to spend the evening with her. They would play cribbage or read together in comfortable companionship, then retire to her bed.

Her first rule remained broken in the dust behind them. Although he did not always stay the night, he often did, and she offered no rebuke except to tell him there would be no breakfast for him. He always took this in good spirit.

He even paid the most pressing of her debts with no complaint. She sold the diamonds Sir Percy had given her, and sent the money into the country. Of course, it could not pay for the dowry, but George's gifts were always extravagant—yet chosen with such care, it pained her to pawn them again.

Still, to her knowledge he was still courting debutantes with the object of marriage; it would not be long until he found a bride and their arrangement would end. She would find another lover to pay for her daughter's dowry—one in whose company she did not find so much enjoyment—and all would go back to how it should be.

Merry widows did not fall in love. It was unbecoming.

That was when disaster struck.

She had known her monthly courses were approaching by the grumbling aches in her abdomen, the pain in her lower back. And so when she awoke to blood between her thighs, she resigned herself to the inevitable and sent a note to George explaining that she would be indisposed. But that was not the problem—if anything, she was relieved at the opportunity for some space.

No, the problem arose when she, in bed with hot chocolate and a fashion plate she was flicking listlessly through, was informed that Mr Comerford had come for her.

She snapped her jaw shut, irrationally irritated. "Come for me? In which respect has he *come* for me?"

"I don't know, my lady. He asked if he could see you."

"I'm indisposed."

"So I told him, my lady, but he insisted on seeing you."

"Did he?" She gritted her teeth, but underneath that was a curiosity that would not be appeased. "Very well. Show him up."

"Yes, ma'am." The maid curtsied and left the room; shortly after, George entered.

"What are you doing here?" she demanded. "You may be inclined to satisfy yourself with me, but I confess I am not."

A smile spread across his face as he stood beside her bed. "Is that what you thought I came here for?"

"What else?" She held up her fashion plate. "I'm afraid I'm otherwise engaged today."

"My poor darling. Does it hurt very much?"

She speared him with a glare. "As though you could imagine it."

"No, very likely not. I brought you some strawberries." He held up a brown paper bag. "And to request the pleasure of your company."

"My company? I thought we agreed that we should not be seen together."

"You stated; I did not agree or disagree." He perched on the bed beside her, removing a strawberry from the bag and offering it to her. "Are you partial to strawberries?"

"I don't understand." She rubbed at her forehead, wishing her headache would ease. "Why have you brought me strawberries?"

His smile was amused. "Do you think me ignorant of women? I suspected what was afflicting you when you asked for a week's break."

"That doesn't explain this." She gestured at the strawberries. "Or your sudden intention of spending time with me."

"I happen to like both," he said, shrugging and biting the strawberry, white teeth breaking through the soft, red flesh. The sight was oddly erotic, and she found herself absurdly wishing she was not on the heaviest, and worst, day of her monthly courses. He grinned at her expression of consternation. "Don't worry, love. I did not come here with an ulterior motive."

That was not the reason for her frown; the reason was that he evidently intended to take her out. And she *wanted* him to.

Foolishness.

She could not bring herself to deny him.

"Where would we be going?" she asked.

"Hampstead Heath," he answered immediately. "I have a picnic made up. We will have nothing to do but sip champagne and sit in the sun—or the shade."

"I don't wish to walk far."

"Then we won't stray far from the carriage."

She narrowed her eyes. "Is this not the behaviour a gentleman should show towards his future wife?"

His grin deepened, and he leant in, one hand coming to her chin. "Such a sharp tongue," he mused. "It's fortunate it feels so good on my—"

She tossed a pillow at him. "Out."

He rose and walked to the door. "By the by," he said, pausing, "it's evident you married young, or you would have known that a young lady of Quality *never* travels unaccompanied with a gentleman to a place such as Hampstead Heath, whether they are due to marry or not." He clucked his tongue. "Really, you ought to have known that, my love."

Her next pillow hit the door.

The trouble was, Caroline enjoyed his company. So many other gentlemen of her acquaintance bored her, but George never supposed she would be disinterested in subjects such as history or politics. When his eyes lit as he spoke to her about the advancement of the Ancient Greeks, she fancied she could sit and listen to him for days at a time. His knowledge also reinvigorated her desire to learn. As a girl, her education had been limited to French and Italian, how to embroider and dance and play the harp. The polite forms of conversation.

Not once had her governess sat her down and told her about the forces at play in Europe at large, or the true cause of the French Revolution. Perhaps it had been too fresh in people's minds, too early for its discussion when she had been a child. But George spoke on the subject with abandon, not once giving her leave to suspect he thought her incapable of keeping up, or that such matters were not a woman's domain.

He was also kind, helping her into the carriage without comment despite her slowness, and sweeping her into his arms when they arrived so she would not have to walk. Servants had already arrived, laying blankets on the soft grass, and a parasol had been erected so she could avoid the sun if she wished. She positioned herself underneath it, and allowed herself to breathe the hot summer air, the fragrance of honeysuckle sweet on the faint breeze.

Beside her, George lounged easily, leaning back on his elbows, the full force of the sun on his face. He squinted into the light.

"You'll get wrinkles if you do that for long," she said, amused. Already, the pain in her lower stomach was easing.

Perhaps it was the sense of peace that surrounded her; so rarely did she come to the country that even its likeness could bring her joy.

"So be it." He closed his eyes entirely. "What does it matter if I do?"

"You'll age faster."

"So? I'm not afraid of my years, or how I wear them."

"A noble sentiment."

"Is that why you aren't enjoying the heat of the sun? I assure you, it's very pleasant."

"I freckle if I'm in the sun too long, and a tan is most unbecoming on a lady."

"I happen to like it," he said, and tugged at her hand, pulling her so she was curled against his side, her palm flat against his chest. She could feel the slow, steady pulse of his heart. "Freckles are not a heinous crime, and neither is a slight browning of your skin."

He was right: the sun was pleasing. She stretched like a cat, and his arm tightened around her waist. "Very well," she murmured. "But when I can find no one else to take me to bed, I shall hold you accountable."

A hard note entered his voice. "I would rather not think of anyone else taking you to bed."

"Jealous, darling?" She laughed softly. "First you must marry."

"A prospect that is less appealing by the day." He paused, and his fingers ran soft circles along the back of her hand. "Why do you always bring up the subject of my future wife?"

Tension entered her body, cramping her still further, and she loosed a breath from between her teeth. "Because this must end, and neither of us should forget it."

"I find things are less enjoyable when you look ahead of them to their demise."

That was entirely the point: she could not allow herself to become too attached to him. But the sun was hot against her cheek, and she was feeling too lethargic to argue with him. Instead, she placed her palm against his jaw, feeling the tiniest prick of stubble against her skin. He was warm and soft, and he turned his head so he could kiss her palm.

"You should not have brought me here today," she said, languorous and content. "But I'm glad you did."

He hummed, deep in his chest, and the sound vibrated through her. It was all too easy to close her eyes and give way to the quiet pleasure of his company, without thought of the future. Her obligations loomed, but he was warm and solid underneath her, and he had brought her strawberries, and it had been a long time since she had felt so drowsily contented.

"Tell me something," he said, fingers trailing to her elbow and back down.

"What?"

"Something no one else knows."

"Hmm?" She toyed with the buttons of his waistcoat. "What makes you think I keep secrets?"

"A lady always has her secrets."

And she had so many.

But as tempting as it was to reveal the worst of hers, she couldn't risk it.

"Let's see," she said, keeping her voice light. "When I was five, I escaped my nursemaid and, by some luck or terrible fortune, found a chicken and stole it."

He laughed, raucous and unashamed. "How did your nursemaid react?"

"Oh, she was furious. But I would not relinquish my prize until my father came to scold me for it." She sighed, recalling his anger at her unladylike behaviour. "I was a trial as a girl. More so as I grew."

"I wish I had been there to see it."

"You don't. I was a termagant."

"I expect I would still have found you divine," he said, his hand sliding to her rump.

"I would not have looked at you twice."

He laughed, throwing his head back. Caroline watched him, fighting her own smile, wishing she did not find so much joy in his. "And who, pray, did you look at twice?" he asked, recovering himself. "I presume, then, there *was* a gentleman."

"Of a kind," she murmured, thinking back to the way the young man had looked at her, arrogant and proprietorial. At seventeen, she had already shared kisses with a few of the young men in her village, and she thought she knew what it was to tease and flirt. In short, she had been as foolish as many a young girl was, and she had paid the price.

"Oh? A farmer's boy?"

"Oh no, darling. He was a lord, but he was not—decidedly not—a gentleman."

He tensed a little under her. "Tell me."

"He was young. Charming enough, at first. They all are, I suppose, and I was an easy target. Not so difficult to seduce, if you can believe."

He was still, save for the fingers that still coasted up and down her arm. "How old were you?"

"Seventeen."

"Ah." The sound was light, but she heard something stir under it. "I think I understand. Was he cruel to you?"

"Only in the way all irresponsible youths are," she said, trying not to let her hurt show. The little lording who had taught her what it was to love, then summarily abandoned her. "But he was kind in other ways. The first to want me exactly as I am."

"Hardly a surprise," George murmured, but to her surprise, he rose, easing her up too until she sat in the gap between his legs. His hands were on her arms still, and his gaze was on hers, eyes that were usually a dancing blue now a deep navy, his brows pulled low. He was usually such an easy-going man, she had forgotten he could look like this—as though revenge was not a concept he was wholly unfamiliar with.

An unsettling feeling slid down her spine. "Don't look at me like that," she whispered.

"Did he force himself on you?"

"No. Heavens, no, George. I am not some poor, hard done by maiden. I offered myself to him, and he accepted with open arms." She had offered, and he had taken, and taken, and taken, and the only thing he had given her in return was a few moments of pleasure—and consequences.

"I was young and foolish," she said, but he pressed a finger against her lips.

"And he? Was he a young man as naïve as you?"

Of course he had not been. Another draw, that a man from London might want *her*.

"I knew what I was doing," she said, holding his gaze. "Or at least, I thought I did."

His jaw was tight, the usual careless disarray of his hair now endearingly soft in contrast to the rigid anger on his face. "Don't excuse him," he said tightly. "Who is he?"

"You are not my defender, George."

"I would be, if only you would let me. Who is he? Give me a name."

"And what would you do with one? Confront him? Accuse him of stealing the innocence of a woman known for bedding half of London?" She laughed then, though he did not. "It would be foolishness, darling, and you know it."

"What does it matter that you've been with men since?"

"It matters because in the eyes of the *ton* I am already fallen." She spoke gently, seeing he really was outraged on her behalf. "And because I was also to blame."

He took her hand and pressed her knuckles to his lips in an oddly tender gesture. They were too often tender with one another, and it frightened her. "Did he hurt you?"

The urgency in his voice was disorienting. Her lovers were not supposed to rise to her defence like knights on white horses, leaving their round tables in search of monsters to vanquish.

He should not have done. He was a poet, a man who made battle with his pen, not his fists.

"Don't," she whispered.

He frowned, looking as though he might say something in response, and she shook her head. Her heartbeat trembled her body, and she felt as though she might split into a dozen tiny pieces and he would scoop them all up in his hands, as though they were precious. As though, to him, *she* was precious.

She had been selling his gifts to provide for her illegitimate daughter. How could she confess to such a thing?

"Caro," he said, the name falling from his lips like honey. Her stomach dipped unsettlingly. "You can be open with me."

"Nonsense," she said lightly. "If I am to compel you to still visit me, I can never be open with you again. A lady must have her secrets."

"Even from me?"

"Oh, darling." She kissed him on the mouth, light as butterfly wings. "*Especially* from you."

Chapter Eight

George sat at his usual table in White's and watched as his friend Henry Beaumont, Viscount Eynsham, settled into the seat beside him. Recently married, Henry had only just returned to London, a fact that was particularly well timed: George was in the unusual position of needing advice.

"You look well," he said.

Henry smirked. "I hear marriage can do that to a man."

"Only if he is attached to his wife first, I fancy."

"Perhaps." Henry shrugged. "Louisa says she hopes she can meet with you in the next few days as well."

"I hope so too." George hesitated, but while his friend was perhaps not the most experienced, he needed to talk to someone. "I have a question."

"Oh?"

"You recall Lady Augustus Spenser?" At his friend's blank look, he added, "Caroline."

A knowing smile crept onto his friend's face. "Ah yes, I remember."

George recalled the time he had swept the papers from his father's desk so he could lay Caroline down on it, and how just a few hours later, he had consoled Henry's broken heart there. "Yes," he said a little hastily. "Well, the problem is that my father is keen for me to marry. Caroline has said herself that she would not do, and I confess that she would not be the logical choice."

"I see," Henry said.

"But once I marry, she will no longer see me."

Henry's brow quirked. "Very honourable of her."

"Very obstinate." George sighed. "My father is dying, and there is nothing anyone can do to stop it. When he does, I will be the Viscount Worthington, and my wife will be a viscountess."

"I understand how these things work," Henry said dryly. "So you are reluctant to choose a wife when it would mean losing Caroline, but you are under obligation to your father."

"Precisely."

"What would you like my advice on?" Henry rested his ankle on his knee, giving George a look of repressed amusement. "How to live with heartbreak?"

"Nothing so tragic. Just—how does one satisfy oneself with choosing a wife when she will not be half the woman you will lose?"

"Why not marry Caroline?"

George's teeth knocked against the glass.

He'd imagined it, of course. Imagined asking her to be his wife, the things she might say. None, at present, seemed especially encouraging. And there was his reputation to think of—Caroline's dealings were well known across the *ton*. She was not bride material, and she knew it as well as he. Plus, given her age of five-and-thirty, there was a chance she might never produce him an heir, the primary reason his father was requiring him to marry.

Even a few weeks ago, he might have laughed at the idea he would consider an action likely to garner so much disapproval. His ideal wife came from a good family with old money and an ancestral seat that went back generations. She would be demure, pretty, and unobtrusive.

Caroline was none of those things. She was hard-headed, seductive, frequently crude, often radical, and five years his senior. In other words, she was the antithesis of the blushing bride he'd always wanted—and he was alarmingly certain he was falling in love with her.

The worst of it was, he sometimes had a thought that perhaps she might feel the same way. But the frequency with which she brought up his future bride made it certain that she did not expect to be the one he chose.

Quite possibly she did not *want* to be his wife.

The thought was humbling.

"It goes against the grain to admit," he said to his friend, "but she might be the one unattached woman in London who would not have me."

"Have you asked her?"

"Of course not. Do you take me for a fool?"

Henry appeared to consider this. "On occasion," he said. "Have you tried wooing her?"

Something else George was decidedly not an expert in. "I took her on a picnic yesterday."

"She might require a little more persuading."

"That's not precisely my realm of experience. How did you prevail upon Louisa to accept?"

"I didn't," Henry said. "She made the decision on her own."

"Unhelpful. Caroline is unlikely to do the same." She was entirely too independent to even consider relying on him, and he expected she had received more than one proposal in the throes of passion.

Henry linked his fingers and lay them across his chest. "From what I gather, Caroline has no particular desire to marry again. But if she likes you, and if you would offer her security, why would she refuse you?"

"People would talk."

"Does she care about that sort of thing?"

"Not for her sake," George allowed. "But she's mentioned the negative impact of her society on my reputation more than once. And it would be bordering on scandalous to marry her, especially given she's older than me by five years."

"Well, if you want my advice, speak to Louisa about how best to win her over," Henry said. "She'll know better than anyone."

The prospect of speaking to sharp-tongued Louisa about his interest in her closest friend was a daunting one, but Henry was probably right. Caroline was withholding something from him. Every time he delved too deeply into her past life, she closed herself off. Out of respect, he had not made enquiries into her family name—he could not have cared if she came from a pig farmer—but perhaps it behoved him to look into her, if he was to pursue her.

Then there was the matter of his father. The sooner he informed the Viscount that he would not be choosing a wife from Forbes's list, the better. He would be free to pursue the one unmarried woman in all of the *ton* whom, he suspected, he had the least chance with.

He was not sure if he had ever wanted anything more.

George entered the Pump Room in Bath with somewhat less than his usual good temper. The journey had been long, dusty, and hot, and when he had arrived at his father's lodgings, it was to the information that his father was not home.

Impatient, barely pausing to write his name in the visitor's book, he glanced around the large room. The pump was at one end, the orchestra at the other, and parties moved up and down in crowds, not seeming to mind the crush. George, also, would not have minded the crush if it had not been so damned hot. He didn't see why more windows could not be open, or why anyone would want to while away their time in such a godforsaken place.

A gap in the crowds allowed him to see his father, carefully seated to one side in his chair and being served a glass of mineral water by a woman in a cap. George strode to join them, and was greeted by the lady's welcoming smile and his father's distinctly unwelcoming gaze.

"Well?" his father demanded.

"What a truly horrific place," George remarked. "I can only be glad you never saw fit to bring me here."

"And I didn't bring you here now," his father said sourly, tossing back the water as though it were brandy. He shuddered. "Awful stuff. What ails you?"

"I've come to inform you that I have chosen a wife."

"About damn time." The irritability in his father's voice didn't waver, but there was finally a burst of interest in his eyes as he waved George to the empty chair beside him. "Sit, sit. Is she from one of the families Forbes sent you?"

George distantly recalled consigning that missive to the fire. "Ah," he said. "No."

"Oh? Then is she good stock?"

The same capped lady offered George a glass of water and he shook his head. "As to that," he said, examining the shine in his boots that had been sadly dimmed by the dust, "I am unsure."

"You don't know her name?"

"Not her maiden name."

"She was married?"

"Yes, sir."

His father's gnarled knuckles whitened as his fingers clenched around the blanket on his legs. "Good God, boy, have you forgotten yourself?"

"I trust I have not."

"A widow to be your wife, the future Viscountess Worthington?" He gave an angry laugh. "What, does she bear your child and want your name for it? Stupid chit. I won't have it."

George's nostrils flared as he struggled to keep his temper. "I would recommend you do not speak ill of her. No, she does not bear my child, but if she did, I would most certainly do the honourable thing."

"Then what is it? Who was her husband? Surely you haven't fallen in love with the girl?"

"Not so much a girl, Father. She is five-and-thirty."

"What is this madness?"

George gave a thin smile. "I mean to have her if I can."

"How so? Has she bewitched you?"

That, George thought, was entirely possible.

"She is as yet unaware of my intentions. I came to inform you first, as I felt was your right."

Spittle flecked the corners of his father's mouth. "Who is she?"

"Lady Augustus Spenser." Her full title, her dead husband's name, sat unpleasantly on his mouth, and he understood anew why she had urged everyone with whom she had an acquaintance to use her Christian name. Far better she offer that intimacy and be addressed by the name she owned, rather than the one she had been forced to use.

"Lady Augustus?" His father's face tightened still further. "That—that *whore*?"

George sat very still in his chair, seconds away from striking his own father. "You will not refer to her in those terms."

"You can't be serious," his father said, still flushed with anger. "Everyone knows she has fewer morals than a gutter rat, and she might have married the younger brother of a duke, but consequence can't shield her now. If you marry her, you will risk ruining our good name."

"If she consents to marry me, then I will be a lucky man indeed, and you will treat her to the respect she is due."

"If you marry her, I won't receive her. Either of you."

George curled her lip. "A coward's answer."

"I mean it, George. Marry her, and I will write you out of my will. I won't have your bastards inheriting the Worthington title, and you may be certain that she won't break the habit of a lifetime and only warm your bed." He coughed into his handkerchief, thin shoulders shuddering. "I've never known you to be so foolish."

George relaxed back into the chair, flicking a speck of dust from his sleeves. "Is that your final say on the matter?"

"I should think so. Marry her, and you won't see a penny."

"Thank you for making the matter so clear, Father." He rose and bowed. "Forgive me for taking up so much of your time."

"What are you going to do? Answer me, or by God I will call my solicitor."

George ignored him. Let him call his solicitor, if that's what he wanted; let him give his fortune to someone else. He had a reasonable independence that would allow him to live comfortably, and if he must sell himself into marriage to inherit, he did not want the money.

But no matter what, whether she married him or no, he would find a way to keep Caroline Spenser.

Chapter Nine

Caroline hadn't expected to miss George the way she did. After the picnic, she didn't see him for another four days, during which point she started to wonder if the distance had made him lose interest. This was, naturally, the best-case scenario, but the pinching sensation in her chest didn't feel like best case.

When she sought out books on Greek plays so she might discuss them with him when he visited her again, she knew things were worse than she ever could have imagined.

To act as an equilibrium, she took some of his more outrageous gifts and pawned them, sending the money into the countryside. That, unsurprisingly, made her feel no better. This was the first time she had ever felt guilty for selling another man's gifts. Usually, she was offered gifts as a form of payment; their arrangement was transactional. Yes, she enjoyed it, and had she enjoyed a little more wealth she would have taken lovers regardless, but she knew they were paying for the pleasure of her company.

George, she knew, was giving her things because he wanted to see the joy they brought her. Items that were not merely expensive fripperies, but things explicitly in her style, or that he thought she would like.

That was what made parting with them so hard.

That, and because she found herself ridiculously attached to the items in question.

It was madness.

But nothing, not even poetry, could soothe the ache his absence left behind.

On the fourth day, the madness infected her brain, and she could not have stayed away even if she had wanted to. Whether she was going to end their arrangement or claim his attention, she didn't know, and still didn't when she arrived outside his house to find his carriage on the street.

"Here for Mr Comerford?" his valet asked, holding the front door open for her. She smiled quickly at him, ducking inside, and came face to face with George. He looked tired, his coat a little creased from having sat in the carriage, and his face careworn. At the sight of her, a wide smile broke across his face.

"Caro," he said, catching her around the waist and pulling her close. The valet disappeared through a door behind them, his butler melted away as though he had never been there, and suddenly it was the two of them again.

Caroline fisted her hands in his waistcoat. No, now was not the time to end their arrangement; perhaps she was condemning her heart, but so long as he remained unmarried, she would continue to see him.

"Did you walk here?" he asked.

"Yes."

"What for?" He tweaked her chin. "I was intending to come and see you tonight."

"I could hardly have known that without prior warning."

"No," he murmured, brushing her flyaway hair from her face. "Am I to infer that you missed me?"

"Stop asking such ridiculous questions and kiss me."

He laughed, but then he was tugging at the ribbons of her bonnet, dragging it roughly from her head and pressing her against the door. His mouth settled on hers, demanding and biting, and it was as though the tension in her body simultaneously loosened and tightened. She was beer in a stopped bottle, shaken and frothing, fizzing with urgency and need.

"You did miss me," he said, dragging her skirts to her hip. "Admit it."

"Never."

"Why else would you be here?"

"I have an obligation to fulfil."

"Is that so?" Without warning, he picked her up, carrying her through to the drawing room and depositing her on the low sofa there. As she lay back, catching her breath, he closed the curtains and returned to kneel before her.

"Next time," he said with a dark smile, pushing her skirts up to her waist, "I will not wait the week."

"Excuse me?"

"You heard." His finger found her slick centre, and his lips curved into a satisfied smile. "If you want me, Caroline, you can have me. Whenever you want, no matter what your body is doing."

She rolled her hips against his fingers, urging him inside. He needed little convincing. "Don't you mind the mess?"

"I'll bathe you before and after." His mouth followed his finger, and she bit her lip at the hot lick. "Have sheets put down."

"I pity the servants who have to wash them."

He nipped the skin at her thigh. "I pay my staff well."

There was too much about this conversation to disturb her—the assumption that in a month, this arrangement would be continuing, his arrogant assurance that they would be doing this act in his home, that she would even consent to him touching her then—but she couldn't focus on them when his busy hands were wreaking such havoc across her body.

And his tongue.

He knelt before her, one hand cupping the pale flesh of her bare thigh, fingers sinking into her skin, his other hand working her. He was everywhere at once, and her head spun with need. Her heart kicked as he drew her into his mouth and sucked.

"Yes," she gasped. "There."

He barely so much as paused to breathe, or so it seemed to her, as though he was somehow as hungry as her. As though he needed to see her fall apart as much as she needed to do the falling.

His fingers plunged into her one last time, hitting right where she needed, and she shattered so completely, she became mindless. His name was on her tongue—she had been calling it, begging and cajoling and gasping, whispering it in the throes of her climax as though their joining meant something more than pure pleasure.

If he suspected the turmoil of her mind, he never said so, merely rising up her body to press a kiss against her mouth, letting her taste herself on his lips. "There," he said, fingers curling around the hinge of her jaw. "Is that better, love?"

Frighteningly so. Internally shaken, she forced a teasing, indulgent smile to her lips and nodded at his breeches. "For me, perhaps, but not for you."

"That's not necessary."

"On the contrary." She was losing control, and this was the only way she could think to regain it. "Allow me." With a low, wicked laugh, she urged him onto a seat and sank to her knees before him. He was already erect, and it was easy to unbutton the fall of his trousers and take him into her mouth. Deep. He groaned, thrusting reflexively, and sank his hand into her hair. Not to guide her movements, but to hold her there as he rocked into her.

Perhaps he had thought he could go without, for whatever misguided reason, but this proved otherwise.

She should not have delighted in it.

She opened her mouth, relaxed her throat, and let him use her as he would. Her submission was a sign of her trust in him, and she knew he understood it even as it aroused him. In his everyday life, he was the usual indolent lord, but when it came to pleasure, he preferred to hold the reins. And she liked the way he found his pleasure in her, the sensation gratifying in its own right. She loved the way her eyes watered, the way he praised her even as he demanded more from her.

Her own pleasure built again, and she reached down her body to her core, touching herself as he guided her head down on him, pushing himself to the very back of her throat, filling her so she couldn't breathe.

"I love seeing you like this," he said, easing free. "Do it again."

She obliged, taking him as deep as she could. On her knees before him, rubbing frantically, wanting to find completion before he did. As though sensing it was a competition, he gave a gritty laugh and loosened her hair from its pins, wrapping it around his fist as he moved her up and down.

Tears streamed down her face, her nose stung, and she was so lost to pleasure she could have drowned in it.

Her climax hit with almost terrifying intensity. It was impossible to moan around him, but she tried, shuddering and gasping, her body another beast entirely, out of her control.

He thickened in her mouth as he slowed, giving her time to breathe and recover. Distantly, she knew that he was close, throbbing and needy. But he waited until she dropped her hands from herself, and then he nodded from his position on the sofa.

"Hands behind your back, Caro."

She obeyed, locking her fingers around her other wrist.

"Now take me," he commanded, and thrust into her mouth. Relaxing her throat, she gave herself over to him utterly, and it only took a matter of seconds before his breathing shattered. She looked up at him as he moaned her name and spilled himself down her throat.

In the early hours of the morning, George lay on his side, Caroline's back against his chest, and wondered how he should go about proving to her that he would make a good husband—and that she was the only wife he had any desire for.

Marrying for love had once been a pipe dream, but she could make it a reality, if only he could persuade her to accept she loved him in return.

Seeing her here when he had returned from Bath had proven to him that her feelings ran deeper than she would confess, and it gave him hope that she would accept.

"Where were you?" she asked sleepily.

"Hmm?"

"When you were gone. Where did you disappear to?"

"I went to Bath."

"Oh?"

"My father lives there."

She stiffened a little. "I see."

"I'm sorry for leaving no note, love." He kissed her hair and inhaled the scent of her. There was nothing so right as the feel of her here in his arms. But much as he enjoyed her in his bed—and he enjoyed that a lot—he wanted her on his arm. For her to bear his name and wander his library as though she owned it, asking him questions that made him pause to think. He wanted every day of challenge that a life with her would bring.

And in return, he wished to remove any burdens that sat on her shoulders. Perhaps the world was not equal, but he could do that for her, at least. Even without his father's fortune at his heels.

"You don't need to apologise," she said, but instead of settling beside him again, she sat up, drawing the sheets around herself. Her blonde hair was ruffled, her curls tangled and in glorious disarray. He adored every knot he had put there. "I don't own you or your time."

He gave her a lazy smile. "On the contrary, my sweet. You have but to crook your finger and I will come."

"Be serious."

"I'm perfectly serious. You are the sun to my moon—I would not glow without your light. I adore you." He said the words lightly, not wanting to scare her too much. "Come back to bed, love."

"Perhaps I shouldn't have stayed."

"Nonsense. Why must you fight this, Caro?"

"Because I cannot bear to grow accustomed to you only to lose you." She sat very straight. "And I will lose you, George. That's the nature of these things."

"Must it be?"

"Yes." Her tone was firm. "We both knew the score before we ever embarked on this agreement. I set boundaries—I established rules. When you are married, this ends." She frowned. "Your father must be very ill if you visited him in Bath."

George took a long breath. "No more ill than before. Death has come knocking, but I doubt he will answer the door just yet. He has too much spite to die."

"That changes very little except the timeline."

"What if there were no timeline?" he asked, looking at her steadily.

"There must be! That's your duty as heir. It's—it's expected. And your father—"

He would rather not think of his father at present. "Let us set aside his expectations for now. Allow me to be honest with you, Caroline. I have no desire for our arrangement to cease. And if you will not consent to being my wife, then—"

"Your wife?" she interrupted, sliding off the bed and taking the blanket with her, still held against her chest although he knew she had no aspirations to modesty. The sight stung. "Why in heaven's name would you think I would marry you?"

This was not how he had envisaged his first proposal going. At the very least, he had imagined flowers, and a marginally more positive answer. "Is the idea of marrying me so repulsive?"

"It's—it's ludicrous. Consider. What will your father say?"

"My father," he said through teeth that were suddenly gritted, "has already said all there is to say on the matter."

"You have already asked him?"

"Informed him, rather. Regardless of what you think, I do not require my father's permission."

She stared at him through wide, grey eyes. He had never seen her look like that, fragile in an indescribable way, as though he had sliced through every layer of defensive sensuality to find her softly beating heart. "But he cannot have taken it well."

"Not well," he conceded. "He threatened to cut me off if I married you, but I care little for that. After I heard what he had to say on the matter, he lost all rights to my respect."

She shook her head, slowly at first, then faster. "George you must—I'm sorry, but I *cannot* marry you."

Chapter Ten

The worst part was, Caroline was tempted.

After her husband's death, she had never once been inclined to marry again. Her lifestyle was unorthodox, but she had chosen it, and she was happy to maintain her independence the way she saw fit. Jacqueline's payments had placed an extra burden on her shoulders, but she had been willing to bear it.

Then George disrupted her routine. He infiltrated not just her bed but her life, her peace of mind. He seduced her in every conceivable way, and the only way to have him was to embrace poverty. To ruin him and her daughter in one fell swoop.

Yet she could see it now, a life with George. Picnics in the country, laughter and desire and the kind of happiness she had once dreamt she could have with another gentleman. And she wanted it. The life she had been denied at seventeen.

It felt like a farce. A joke. Fate laughing in her face as it ripped the one thing she had ever wanted since the boy who ruined her first.

Panic turned the corners of her vision black as she fought to keep her head. This should not be happening; he should not have fallen in love with her. He should not want her, when she was five years his senior and could not be guaranteed to produce him another child.

Cruel of him to ask her when it would be harming his reputation.

Yet if it were not for Jacqueline's dowry, she might have accepted.

Clearly, she was out of her mind.

"Caro?" George touched her face, and when she blinked, he was before her, naked and glorious, and she loved him. She ached with it.

"This should have ended long ago." Her voice didn't sound like her own. "That was my error."

"End? Surely not." The hurt in his eyes filled her vision. "If you won't be my wife, then continue to be my mistress."

"It's a flattering offer, but no." She hunted for her clothes. Why had she let him remove them from her and cast them about the room in all directions? "I have—I have obligations. Things I must . . . and you must marry a wife better suited to you."

"There is no one more right for me than you."

"Nonsense." She laughed, but the sound was brittle, and heavens, she felt as though she was breaking apart. "You missed me and are blinded by post-coital bliss, but your father was right: I would not make you a good wife. Think of the scandal."

"Are *you* afraid of it?" he asked, looking at her intently.

"Not for me, but for you. What viscount marries his whore? Think, George."

"Many a man across history has married his mistress," he said, cupping her jaw in his hand. "There may be a small scandal, but the *ton* will recover, and it will all be forgotten. You never told me who you were before you married, but you are Lady Augustus Spenser, and you married the son of a duke. Nothing about you is beneath me."

"So many things about me are beneath you."

"Then tell me them."

She should, perhaps. Hammer the final nail into her coffin and confess to Jacqueline. Instead, she reached a hand to her bare throat; she wore no jewels. "I sold everything you gave me," she said, and watched as confusion crossed his face. "Every last piece that you chose for me so carefully." Her breath was harsh, and she was going to have to be careful or she might cry. "They are gone. Do you not see? I cannot marry a poor man, and I will not give my heart to a man who will marry another." Not again. She dashed a hand across her eyes as she buttoned up her dress poorly. Never mind—her pelisse would cover it. All she cared now was about leaving. "It's better this way. Believe me. You'll forget me soon, and then you will be glad I had the sense to refuse you."

His eyes were dark, the expression pained. "There is nothing about this that I will look back on with thankfulness."

There was nothing more to say. For the second time in her life, Caroline had fallen in love, and she wished she might have done it with a less honourable man so she could have the luxury of hating him in peace.

As it was, she had nothing and no one but herself to blame.

Caroline had forgotten she and Louisa had planned on visiting the Royal Academy until she heard her friend stride through the house as though she owned it.

"In here, darling," she called, pushing herself up from her reclined position on the sofa. The half-opened bottle of sherry was on the table before her, and she took hold of it, pouring herself a glass.

Louisa swept into the room and stopped. She frowned. "You look dreadful."

"You are always a balm to my wounded feelings."

"What happened to wound your feelings?"

Caroline was not a lady, and she did not succumb to lady-like habits; she tossed back her thimbleful of sherry. "George proposed," she said shortly.

"Oh no."

"Yes."

Louisa sank into the sofa beside her. "And you refused him?"

"Must you really ask me that question? I am not so far gone that I would let him waste away his life with me." Caroline wished she were in the mood for cake. Everything would be easier if she could eat her feelings into oblivion. Sadly, the very prospect of food made her feel ill. Hence the sherry.

Good decisions had never been her forte.

Louisa's eyes were still wide. "Is he in love with you?"

"That's what he claims," Caroline said, pouring herself another drink. "Would you like one?"

"It's ten in the morning, dearest."

"Is it? I barely slept, so I suppose I have the luxury of classing today as last night still."

Louisa looked at her with amusement. "So you love him too, do you?"

"You warned me I would fall in love and regret it, and you were right." The lesson had been a cruel one, but she would learn from it. In time. "I love him far too much to marry him."

"That logic is faulty and you know it."

"That's because I never told you the full of it." Caroline reclined again, her head spinning and her body aching. Age, that was what it was—growing old was an indignity. "For the past ten years, I have been funding my daughter's dowry and living situation."

To her credit, Louisa barely blinked. "You have a daughter?"

"Not Augustus's," Caroline hastened to clarify. She had not become with child with her husband, thank the Lord. "Small mercies, I suppose."

"Then whose?"

"No one of concern. He's now middle-aged and lives in the country with his much younger wife; I've had no occasion to meet him in town." Another reason to be thankful, although it hardly felt as though she had amassed all that many. "The fact of the matter is, I am financially responsible for her, and if George were to marry me, his father has threatened to cut him off. I would not have the money to send to Jacqueline, and I could hardly expect him to bankrupt himself for the sake of a child that was never his." She pressed her fingers against her forehead. "It would be easier for him to forget me, and I think it will be easily done once I am not seeing to his needs. He was not thinking clearly."

"I think he is the best judge of that."

Caroline poured herself another glass. "He doesn't know about Jacqueline."

"You never told him?"

"Why should I saddle him with the knowledge of another man's child? Besides, I'm too old for him, and he would be penniless if we married. It's better he forgets me." She waved a hand. "Go, darling. Let me suffer in peace. I will finish this sherry and eat some cake and by the end of it, I will be myself again." And prepared to do whatever she must to secure the future of her daughter.

"You fool," Louisa said as she entered George's breakfast room the day after. "You utter fool, George."

His head ached. After Caroline had left the previous morning, he had over-indulged. As a result, he was not in the mood to entertain Louisa's sharpness.

"Thank you for your consideration," he muttered, sipping his coffee and wishing the world was not so bright.

"Have you no sense?"

"It appears that allowing you entry into my house displays a distinct lack of it."

She ignored him, whirling to the curtains and yanking them open. He squinted in pain at the sudden burst of sunshine. "You deserve that," she informed him. "And more. What were you thinking?"

"Evidently I was not."

"If you were intending to propose, why did you let her think you were penniless?"

"I said no such thing."

"You said your father would cut you off."

"From the bulk of his fortune, certainly, but I have a tidy inheritance elsewhere. It's not a vast fortune, perhaps, but it will suffice perfectly nicely." He squinted at her. "Why, have you spoken with her?"

"We had an engagement—she had forgotten but I had not." She took a seat beside him. "Did she give her reasons for refusing?"

"I gather she thinks she is too old and too notorious." He winced at the memory. "And she has been selling the jewels I bought her."

"Of course she has," Louisa said pragmatically. "How else did you expect her to survive?"

"I told her on more than one occasion that if she wanted for anything, I would provide it. And I thought she was left some money by her late husband? My gifts—they were designed as fripperies, things she could wear to the opera. Not necessities."

Louisa sighed, massaging her eyes. "I had not thought you so foolish."

"What obligations does she have that I was unaware of?"

"Are you in love with her?"

"What an obnoxious question."

"I take it that's a yes."

In the past, a sonnet or two had been enough to bleed his love away, until he had concluded it had not been love at all. Usually, he tired of his lovers within weeks. Caroline was the only one who stayed the night, who awoke sleepily at dawn to climb atop his body. Who, laughing, recited the historical facts he had relayed the night before as she rocked above him, her words devolving into gasps.

"What do you want from me?" he asked wearily. "Yes, I love her. It's entirely possible I've been in love with her since the very first moment I laid eyes on her. I want her to be mine even if it's foolishness and the world turns its back on me—so long as she wants that too."

"Very well, then." She tapped her fingers against the table. "Caroline had a child out of wedlock before she married and moved to London. From what I understand, she has been providing for the girl all these years—and she had too much pride to put the burden of her dowry on you when she learnt you would be cut off from your father."

He froze, the implications of this coming tumbling down around him. The lover from her childhood had left her with his bastard, and she had been picking up the pieces ever since. No wonder she had raged against the injustice of the world when she had been forced to bear its cross.

Relief flooded through him, mingling with his anger. "Did she truly suppose that I was asking her only to drag her into poverty with me?"

Louisa raised a brow. "*You* made it sound like that, George."

"She left before I could explain the terms of my inheritance," he said impatiently. "This daughter—how old is she?"

She shook her head. "I know none of the details. The only reason I'm telling you is because her pride won't let her."

"The little fool. As though I should have balked at providing for her daughter."

"There are other considerations," Louisa reminded him. "She's older than you."

"I care nothing for that." He rested his elbows on his thighs, painful gaze fixed on Louisa. "Tell me, as a friend, how am I to make this right?"

Chapter Eleven

Caroline gave herself one day to grieve the future she should never have wanted, then forced herself back into business. As she was disinclined to take on another lover, she would have to give up her house to pay the next instalment of Jacqueline's dowry. All George's gifts were now gone, swallowed by her need to provide for her child.

Her pride made it impossible to accept Louisa's offer of a house, and Sir Percy was finally reuniting with his wife. Her presence there would be unwelcome at best, though she knew he would never turn her away.

The only other place she had to go was back into the country.

Home.

Decision made, she ordered for her life in London to be packed, and it was done more easily than she could have imagined. Anything she couldn't pack, she sold. Paintings, furniture, clothes; compared to the things she had already lost, this was nothing. Once her servants had finished disposing of it all, they would send her the money, and she would have the luxury of considering her next steps.

Thus, two days after George's ill-timed proposal, she left her London house for the last time, enduring the indignities of a stagecoach until she arrived on her mother's doorstep, a single carpet bag in her hands and nothing else to her name. It was raining.

The last time she had seen this house was when she was eighteen years old and her marriage was being negotiated to a man well past his prime. It had been raining then, too—the universe delighted in irony, it seemed. But even despite the rain, the muted lavender's merry scent from its place by the front door warmed her, and when the housekeeper opened the door, she smiled.

"Hello, Hill," she said. "I have returned."

For a moment, Hill's jaw hung wide. Then she remembered herself and snapped it shut. "Does your mother know?" she asked faintly, holding the door wide so Caroline and her carpet bag could step inside.

"She does not," Caroline said. "Be so good as to inform her."

Hill bobbed what might have been a curtsy and disappeared down the corridor. Caroline removed her bonnet and took off her coat, shaking out the water as she hung it on one of the hooks by the door. The familiarity of the gesture was ironic; she had almost spent half her lifetime away from this place, and yet her body remembered how it had been to live here.

At a noise from the end of the corridor, Caroline looked up to find her mother standing in the gloom, ramrod straight and clutching the locket at her chest. She looked old and frail, not the fiery witch that lived in Caroline's memory.

For a moment, neither woman spoke. They watched each other warily, unsure how the other would react. Finally, her mother stepped forward. "Caroline," she said.

"Hello, Mother."

Her mother's gaze darted to the two large cases by her feet. "Hill," she said, with a tolerable appearance of calm, "take Lady Augustus's luggage to her room."

"Yes, ma'am."

Caroline winced at the sound of her late husband's name, but refused to acknowledge the blow. "Have you eaten yet?" she asked. "I confess I'm famished."

Her mother caught her shoulders, and for an instant Caroline thought she would push her away. Instead, she pressed a dry kiss to her cheek. "I've just started. Sit and tell me why you're here."

A lump rose to Caroline's throat. After her disgrace, she'd had no contact with her mother, in part out of resentment and in part because neither had broken the silence. She hadn't even been certain her mother would accept her presence in the house, but here they were.

Dinner was not lavish; her mother lived alone and was not a heavy eater. Even so, there was enough to satisfy Caroline, and as she began scooping potatoes onto her plate, she said, "I apologise for not sending word of my arrival. My leaving London was somewhat abrupt."

Her mother's ruby earrings quivered in the candlelight. "Are you in disgrace?"

"Not at all. I merely find it difficult to provide for myself without Gus's fortune. You know he left it elsewhere."

Her mother tucked her shawl more tightly around her shoulders. "Is that all? You look . . . tired."

"I am tired, I suppose." Caroline allowed the footman to pour her some wine and raised it, hesitating. The subject of her daughter lay between them, and after a tense moment, she decided to address it. "Jacqueline is going to London next year."

Her mother clung to her glass with white-knuckled determination. This had never been easy for her—born into a deeply religious family, her faith had been her cornerstone, and she had been bitterly disappointed in Caroline's transgressions. Caroline was the antithesis of everything she had believed in, and while she likely did not hold Jacqueline responsible, she had never wanted anything to do with the girl. Jacqueline was a physical representation of Caroline's shame.

But years had passed since that first confrontation, where Caroline had confessed her wickedness and her mother had condemned her. If it weren't for her father's intervention, her mother might have cast Caroline out into the world.

Now, old pain filled her mother's eyes. She closed them briefly, and Caroline wondered if she had pushed too far too soon.

"I know you resent me for what I did," she said.

"I raised you better than to fall into bed with the first gentleman who tempted you." The sharpness in her mother's voice had been worn smooth by age and regret. "You should have known better."

"Oh, Mother."

"You were seventeen—hardly a girl."

"I loved him."

Her mother reached for her locket. "Even so," she said feebly. "You should have known better."

"He promised me marriage and everything else a young man promises when he wishes to get under a lady's skirts." At her mother's flinch, Caroline softened her voice. "Have you never wanted something so badly you would put everything aside for a taste of it? I was young and foolish and I paid the price—more heavily than you'll ever know."

"I've heard rumours of what you do in town."

"Yes." Caroline refused to back down. "Is that wrong? After Father's death, paying for Jacqueline's future fell to me. What else was I to do? Starve for your morals?"

That had certainly been too far. Her mother released a long breath. "Why are you here, Caroline?"

"Because I have nowhere else to go." She glanced to one side, feeling the sting in her nose. Foolish; she never cried. "And because I made the same mistake all over again."

"Are you with child?"

"No, no." Caroline glanced at her hands, the nails she had always taken such pride to keep polished and pretty. Her appearance had always been her greatest asset, but sometimes she thought it a terrible thing to be born beautiful in a world where a woman's consent meant very little. "No, the truth is . . ." She took a breath. "The truth is, Mother, that I have fallen in love. And it has ruined me."

Chapter Twelve

After travelling to Ipswich and setting up a trust for Jacqueline, the remaining portion of her dowry to be paid there instead, Caroline took her horse to Framlingham, where Jacqueline now lived. It was a small village, situated under the shadow of a ruined castle, and the high street consisted of two milliners' shops, a mantua-maker, and several stalls selling bread and fish and meat. A blacksmith's sign creaked in the wind, the sound of hammering metal clanging on the light breeze, and there was an inn at the end of the road that catered to all the few travellers who came to the place. There was also a coffee house within for the locals, Caroline presumed, although she didn't enter. At her age, and a widow, she thought nothing of walking around unchaperoned, but she didn't want to cause any gossip in the town her daughter lived in.

When she'd told her father of her situation—that she was with child—he had searched for a suitable family who might take her in as a ward. The family he had settled on were the Smiths, middle-class enough to have a respectable place in society, but in a position to welcome the financial incentive that accepting Jacqueline would bring.

Over the years, Caroline had suspected that Mrs Smith had grown overly reliant on this financial assistance, and might even have been tempted to use Jacqueline's dowry for her own purposes. However, she had become certain over the years that Mrs Smith had become fond of Jacqueline for her own sake—if not as a child of her own, then close.

Caroline lingered by the curved windows of a milliner's shop, pretending to examine the ugly bonnets inside as she waited. Her heart drummed inside her chest, and more than once, she was forced to wipe her damp hands down her skirts. The heavy June heat made her discomfort worse, and she was beginning to wonder if she had wasted her time when she caught a glimpse of blonde hair on the other side of the road.

The girl was tall, a bonnet's ribbons tied loosely under her chin, and her golden hair fell in loose curls around her face. She was walking with a shorter, slimmer girl perhaps a year or two older, and they had their heads together, laughing. The sounds of their mirth carried across the road, and Caroline stood still in shock as she watched her daughter, Jacqueline, the girl she had given birth to, walk across the road.

She wasn't immediately beautiful; her eyes were a soft brown and a little too large in her face, unbalancing it somewhat. Her nose was a button and her mouth too thin above a strong chin. But her figure was lush and rounded, and the expressiveness of her eyes went a long way to absolve the plainness of her face.

Caroline would have changed nothing about her.

Moving as though in a dream, she followed the two girls along the street, watching from a distance as they turned up a track towards a decently sized house on the outskirts of the city. Perhaps they were not rich, and they had no claim to the aristocracy, but they had enough to be comfortable, and the amount that Caroline had paid every month for the past ten years had no doubt added to their comfort.

All the things Caroline had feared—that Jacqueline would be neglected, unhappy, either too beautiful or too plain, or perhaps compromised herself—had been assuaged. Jacqueline was happy. It was evident she had her 'sister' were close, and by the looks of the baskets under their arm, they had been visiting the poor.

Still laughing, the girls opened the front door, and Caroline held her breath as her first and last glimpse of her daughter came to an end. The door shut behind them, and the two girls were enclosed inside.

She had to fight the urge to go to the door and bang on it, demanding to see her daughter. This was the role she had assigned herself: the one of onlooker. She could never be present and a part of Jacqueline's life. That was the agreement when she had given the girl up at birth.

Her heart hurt. Joy and grief battled for prominence. Jacqueline was happy. Her life was not as privileged as it might have been, but it was comfortable. Caroline could not have asked for more.

And yet she was not hers.

She turned, a hand on her stomach as though to hold herself together, and slowly walked the path back down into the town.

At first, she barely noticed the smart black coach on the other side of the street, and she might have passed it by entirely if a hand had not caught her arm, swinging her around to face him.

"Caroline," George said. "I've been looking everywhere for you."

Chapter Thirteen

George.

George was *here.*

Her George, the man she had come to love with an intensity that scared her, had tracked her down to this tiny town where her daughter lived. It oughtn't to have been possible, and she looked around for an answer. Some reason to his presence here.

At her dumbstruck silence, he smiled. "I see you weren't expecting me."

"You should have been in London."

"I left approximately . . ." He checked his watch. "Eight hours ago."

A carriage was at the other end of the street, four horses waiting patiently in front of it. For him to have reached her by the afternoon, he must have left *very* early.

"Your mother told me where you were," he explained. "Before you fire up at her, she had no intention of doing until

I explained that I knew about your daughter and wished to marry you."

He'd said that to her mother? Her knees felt alarmingly like jelly, and if he had not taken her arm, she might have fallen onto the cobblestones. Everything had happened so fast—and George had found her. Here. Against all odds.

He knew about *Jacqueline.*

"I don't understand," she said. The only phrase she could bring to mind.

"Then let me make everything perfectly clear, Caroline. The last time, you caught me off guard and I fudged things, as Louisa was kind enough to inform me, but this time I shall do things right." His warm blue eyes smiled at her. "If you had stayed a little longer, I might have had a chance to explain that *should* my father cut me off, I will not be destitute. Moreover, given my father's health and decline, I'm confident that we would not lose much by waiting until he passes. There's little he can do to my inheritance from beyond the grave."

"But—"

"I'm not done." He took one of her hands, gloveless, and spread her fingers. "I love you, my stubborn, infuriating darling. And I would marry you in a heartbeat even if you were ten years my senior and had fifteen children."

I love you.

The words scorched her on their way down her throat, as though she was breathing in smoke from a fire.

"Fifteen children would be too many," she said, and sniffed. "But I have a daughter. I was selling your gifts in order to provide for her. Are you not angry?"

He drew her in closer until the heat from his body soaked through her. "Extraordinarily," he said against her hair. "Why did you not tell me immediately? I could have done so much more for her if I had only known."

She pushed back so she could see his face. "You would have provided for my daughter?"

"Did you think I wouldn't? My darling, I have already made arrangements to pay whatever remains of her dowry."

For perhaps the first time in her life, she was speechless. Perhaps she hadn't thought he would reject her outright—he was liberal minded, for a man—but she had never thought he would accept Jacqueline as his own.

"Are you serious?" she managed.

"Utterly. You have consumed my every waking moment since Worthington. I am a man possessed, and a broken heart does me no credit. Louisa informs me I've become gloomy."

All of the things she wanted now within grasp. It seemed too good to be true. Still. For his sake she should advance the last of her arguments. "I'm five years older," she said.

"You don't look a day over twenty."

"You're a liar."

"But a charming one."

That, she couldn't deny. "And what if I am unable to have more children?"

"I've given it some thought and I've decided that I have no need for heirs. Not if I can have you." He made as though to embrace her, but she stopped him with a hand on his chest. People were already staring. "You are not as old as you think you are, Caro. And if we have no children together, at least

I shall have a wife who loves me for more than my title. It's always been a dream of mine, foolish romantic that I am."

She did not think she could love him more. "An honourable dream."

"Will you help it come true?" He pressed her fingers to his lips, the gesture making her heart stutter. Something warm erupted in her belly. "You've been taking care of yourself and everyone else for far too long. Let me take care of you." The corners of his eyes crinkled as he smiled. "So long as you don't object to living in sin first."

Tucking her hand in his arm, she led the way back to his carriage. If they remained in place much longer, she wouldn't be able to resist throwing herself in his arms, and that *would* make people talk. "What about your father?"

"I'll tell Forbes—his butler—to send me another list of eligible females. He'll be delighted that I've come around." His voice was dry. "Meanwhile, I will feed you strawberries and wake up beside you every morning. What more could a man want?"

"I can think of several things," she murmured, sending him a speaking glance that made his eyes flare. A delicious burst of heat crawled across her skin.

There was no way she could deny him now. No further reason she could think of to want to.

"Did you come here in a coach?" he asked.

"I rode."

"Excellent." As they reached his carriage, he clicked his fingers. "Warwick?"

A head poked out from the other side of the horses. "Yes, sir?"

"Lady Augustus has a horse stabled here. Arrange for it to be taken back to Lady Rowland's stables." He reached into his pocket and tossed a coin bag at the man. "Cost is no object."

"Yes, sir."

"Did you see Jacqueline?" George asked as he handed her up into the carriage.

Caroline swallowed the thick, heavy feeling in her throat. "I did."

"And?"

"She looks happy."

"Good." He squeezed her hand. "Then you won't object to bringing her to London next year to stay with us?"

"George—"

"I won't hear any opposition, you know," he said, closing the door behind them and shutting the curtains. "I know you love me."

And she had tried so very hard not to let it show. "You are insufferable," she told him, attempting to make her voice severe.

"Absolutely." He kissed her knuckles again. "But I'm insufferably yours. Now, what do you think to ten thousand?"

"Excuse me?"

"Jacqueline's dowry. Respectable, but not so much that she falls prey to fortune hunters. But enough to overcome any significant doubts about her birth."

"Ten *thousand*?"

"I can afford to, you know," he said.

"It's not a question of whether or not you can afford it, George, but—" She hardly knew where her opposition was coming from. This was everything she had every dreamt of. The security she had not allowed herself to crave.

His smile fell away, and he reached for her, bringing her onto his lap and holding her tight against him. "Let me make one thing plain," he said, kissing her cheek. "If she is yours, then I will love her; and if you wish to provide for her, then I will hand you the means to do so. That is love, Caro."

When Lord Berkley, young and handsome, had whispered lines of adoration to her in the orchard, as he pushed up her skirts and took her against a tree, she had believed it was love. Yet at the first obstacle, when pleasure dissolved into obligation, he fled.

Somehow, George was still here, pressing tender kisses to the side of her face, brushing away her tears with gentle fingers.

"There is nothing you could do to persuade me not to love you," he said, and Caroline gave into the inevitable. She turned her face into his, catching his mouth with her lips, and his hand came to her jaw, holding her against him with just the right amount of pressure.

"How can I say no now?" she asked.

"Frankly, my darling, I hope you won't."

"It won't be easy," she warned, shifting her hips closer to his. "I love you too much to bear you with any lady but me."

"That was not even a consideration."

She kissed along his jaw. "I can be crotchety and demanding."

"As though I was unaware."

She laughed then cupped his face. "And I shall demand strawberries even when they are out of season."

"Then we shall travel to warmer climes." His hand slid down her side, and his thumb dug into the flesh of her stomach, holding her against him so she could feel how aroused he was. Her head spun at the feeling. How long she had been denied—how little she would have to be denied now. "Whatever you need, whatever you want, whatever will make you happy, I will do it."

"Can I deserve you?"

His lips brushed her neck. "I think the real question is whether I can contrive to deserve you."

"Oh, darling." She tipped her head back, giving him access, giving him everything. "You already do."

Epilogue

March 1816

Jacqueline propped her hands on her chin, ignoring the rattling that travelled from the side of the carriage, up the elbow she leant against it, and into the bones of her head. This was the first time she had come to London, and she didn't want to miss a second of it. The noise, the smells, the buildings that all rose so tall about her.

Mrs Smith hadn't wanted her travelling alone, and had thought about refusing to send her at all, but Lord and Lady Worthington had sent a manservant and carriage all the way out to Suffolk, so it was not for them to refuse.

Jacqueline was glad. She'd dreamt of coming to the capital at some point in her life, and although it was a shame dearest Olivia, her sister, could not come with her, she could still hardly contain her excitement. She'd always felt as though the life she had been born into was too small, and now she was finally getting a chance to experience something different. Admittedly, flirting with the curate had been a fun way of passing the time, and she did adore her family, but there were more important things than haggling for the price of fish on market days, or darning socks by the light of an indifferent candle.

London was the place adventures happened. Her veins were fairly fizzing with it.

As they passed through the outskirts of London, they came across even larger houses. There were gated parks and shops selling all things. It was fascinating. And the people! Jacqueline had never seen so many people in one place in her life. Tradesmen with their wares; ladies lifting their skirts over puddles; skinny children dressed in rags, slipping through the crowds with their quick hands.

Then, as they reached the heart of London, it became ladies with heavily embroidered shawls and liveried footmen with packages, and so many carriages it was a struggle for Jacqueline's groom to navigate the busy streets.

Finally, they came to a street—she did not know which, they all looked the same to her—lined by tall, pale houses with too many windows and black railings leading up to the front door.

So this was where she was to be staying.

She'd known that Lord and Lady Worthington were wealthy, but she hadn't known the extent of it. The building went on for what felt like miles on either side. And there was nothing green to be seen: no garden with buzzing bees and gradually unfurling flowers. There was nothing here but exquisite stonework and a certain sense of grandiose that made her feel as though she had left the country a long way behind.

Briefly, nerves overcame her excitement, but then a footman was emerging from the front door and letting down the steps of her carriage, and when she glanced up, it was to see Lady Worthington herself in the doorway. Instead of the austere lady she had been envisaging—Mrs Smith had said not to expect anything from her; the nobility were notoriously fickle—she was beaming, dressed in a becoming green dress that hugged her curves, and her blonde hair set stylishly below a hat with a long feather.

"Darling," she said, coming down the steps to greet Jacqueline. "I'm so glad you made it safe and unharmed." She peered into the carriage's interior. "Have you no maid?"

"Mrs Smith said she could not spare Nancy," Jacqueline said, unsure whether this was a faux pas immediately on meeting her host. But although Lady Worthington's face briefly seemed to tighten, her expression soon dissolved into another smile.

"Never mind that—you can use my maid until we find you one. Now come inside, darling. You must meet George."

"George?"

"Lord Worthington." Lady Worthington hesitated as she led Jacqueline into the elegant hallway. "You mustn't stand on ceremony with us, you know. I'm Caroline to all my friends, and I'm determined we'll be friends. Ah," she said as a tall man approached. He was handsome in a careless way that Jacqueline knew from novels denoted someone was high fashion, and he gave Lady Worthington such a look of speaking devotion that it was plain their marriage had been a love match.

Jacqueline felt a slight pang deep in her chest. Not jealousy, precisely, but because she wanted to have that one day. Olivia was in love with the butcher's assistant, but Mrs Smith was insisting on taking her to London to find a better match. Olivia wanted nothing else than to stay home and marry, but the butcher's boy wasn't good enough for her. At least, according to Mrs Smith.

"This is George," Lady Worthington said, laying a hand on the man's arm. He gave her a brief smile, then turned his attention to Jacqueline.

"Pleasure to have you staying with," he said, bowing. "Caro tells me you're being presented?"

"Yes," Jacqueline said, "but I haven't got a court dress. Mrs Smith said that you would be so kind as to—"

"Absolutely." Lady Worthington—Caroline—nodded as she led Jacqueline through to an expansive drawing room. All the rooms here were vast. Far different from the ones at home, even if Mr Smith was a gentleman and they had a carriage. "If there's anything you need, all you have to do is ask."

Jacqueline looked around, then back at Caroline. There was something about the woman's grey eyes and smiling mouth, as though she was familiar in some way, although they looked very little alike. Jacqueline knew she was not objectively pretty; her eyes were expressive and her figure good, but her nose and mouth were too small, and she did not have Olivia's dark beauty.

This woman was fair and lovely in a way that Jacqueline, also fair, was not. Even so, the sense of familiarity persisted, if vague.

"Forgive me," she said, "but Mrs Smith could not tell me precisely in which ways we are related. My parents are dead, but from what I understand, they had no siblings."

Caroline smiled, but it struck Jacqueline as being a little sad. "Your mother and I were best friends, and I always swore to look out for you as best I could. I suppose I thought the best way to do that was by introducing you to London Society. I have lived in it a long time—since I was your age, in fact."

Jacqueline tilted her head, but she couldn't work out how old she thought Caroline was. Perhaps in her thirties, although she looked ten years younger than Mrs Smith, who would be forty in the autumn.

Jacqueline's sense of adventure won out. "Will we go to the theatre? Drury Lane? I have heard such things! Mr Smith went once, and he told us how delightful it is. And the opera. I have a great desire to see the opera."

"You will do all these things and more." A servant entered the room with tea and plum cake. "Sit, please, my dear, and tell me a bit about yourself. My connection with your mother has left me . . . I want to know everything. Has Mrs Smith been kind to you?"

Jacqueline sat and accepted the cup of tea. Her nerves had settled now; she had nothing to fear from the kindness of this woman, and the idea of there being a connection to her mother, no matter how vague, made her want to weep with relief. Mrs Smith had never given her any insight into her family, save that she had none and should not think of them.

As Jacqueline talked about her childhood, the way she had played with Olivia by the pond and the enjoyment she'd had from the local curate's intentions, her love of embroidering and pianoforte and her dislike of singing—"I am unable, ma'am, and that's the truth of it"—Caroline did not appear to lose interest. Her grey eyes shone with an emotion Jacqueline couldn't name, and when she finally ran out of words, she had the impression that Caroline would have listened for many hours more.

"What of you, Lady Worthington?" she asked when she was finished. "I'm sure your life has been far more interesting than mine."

"Interesting?" Caroline gave a low, throaty chuckle, and looked away as George entered the room. Their gazes locked, and although Jacqueline couldn't sense what passed between them, she understood that it was potent. The air itself seemed to crackle. "Yes. I think I would have to agree. Perhaps one day I'll tell you. But for now, would you like some cake?"

Thank you so much for reading His Ample Desire! If you enjoyed it, please consider leaving a rating or review. They mean so much to me as an author!

If you haven't already read the other books in my Finders Keepers series, you can find them here(US) or here (UK). And if you were wondering if Percy and Cecily get their own story, you're in luck! Find their novella here.

And finally, if you would like to read the extended epilogue about Caroline and George's lives in 25 years, sign up to my newsletter here to download and read for free!

About the author

Despite the less-than-warm reception of Terri's early stories about cannibal dwarves and talking wolves, she has been writing almost as long as she has been talking. Regency romance is her passion, fed on a diet of Georgette Heyer and Julia Quinn, and she especially loves an irredeemable rake. By day, she's a ghostwriter, but don't ask her about it because 1) she's not allowed to tell you, and 2) she'll freeze up and forget how to form full sentences.

She lives in England with her sadly redeemable husband and the love of her life (her dog). When she's not writing, she's probably wishing she was.

If you enjoyed her books, rate this book and give her a follow on Facebook or Instagram. Even better, sign up for her newsletter where she'll share bonus scenes, extended epilogues, current reads, promos and more. And it'll mean you're first in line to get advance copies of every book she puts out. Yay!

Printed in Great Britain
by Amazon

62806474R00078